THE L

Also by Terry Grimwood

Interference

THE LAST STAR

TERRY GRIMWOOD

Elsewhen Press

The Last Star
First published in Great Britain by Elsewhen Press, 2023
An imprint of Alnpete Limited

Copyright © Terry Grimwood, 2023. All rights reserved
The right of Terry Grimwood to be identified as the author of this
work has been asserted in accordance with sections 77 and 78 of the
Copyright, Designs and Patents Act 1988. No part of this
publication may be reproduced, stored in a retrieval system or
transmitted in any form, or by any means (electronic, mechanical,
telepathic, magical, or otherwise) without the prior written
permission of the copyright owner.

Elsewhen Press, PO Box 757, Dartford, Kent DA2 7TQ
www.elsewhen.press

British Library Cataloguing in Publication Data.
A catalogue record for this book is available from the British Library.

ISBN 978-1-915304-27-8 Print edition
ISBN 978-1-915304-37-7 eBook edition

Designed and formatted by Elsewhen Press

Dedicated to:

Harry, the newest member of the clan. You've started out on the voyage, little fella, travel safely.

And to Professor Brian Cox, who's intensely moving exploration of space and time in his TV series *Universe* was the inspiration for this tale.

AUTHOR'S WARNING

Dear Reader

While *The Last Star* is a science fiction novella, it is not *hard* science fiction. I have attempted to give it authenticity by adhering to some basic principles of astrophysics, cosmology and space travel, but have also stirred a great deal of artistic licence into the mix. The prime motivator behind *The Last Star* is to tell a story, to give the reader a sense of wonder and to ask a question or two. So, thank you for opening this book and I hope your journey into the everlasting out-there is an enjoyable one.

Kind Regards

Terry Grimwood

PART ONE

Subjectively, it was the blink of an eye. A few seconds of claustrophobia as the lid slid shut on the stasis tank. A moment of panic in the coffin-like darkness. The sting of the anaesthetic then, almost immediately, or so it seemed, light, disorientation and an exhaustion that belied the body's extended inactivity and non-being.

Nauseated, dizzy, and dazzled by the lighting in the *Drake's* deep-space travel module, Mission Commander Lana Reed almost found herself yearning for another period of premature burial in the tank. Her head pounded under the jackhammer assault of a migraine. She trembled as she gently withdrew the anaesthetic and IV needles from the back of her hands and made the final disengagement from the tank's life support system. She took a steadying breath then she eased herself to her feet.

For a moment it felt as if the skin suit was the only thing that held her together and kept her upright. Which puzzled her. She had been through stasis before and never felt this weak and unwell afterwards. Atrophy suppressants were included in the cocktail of meds and chemicals poured in, and drained out of, her system. These were supplemented by an electrical massage function which prevented muscle wastage and bone loss during pre- and post-stasis unconsciousness. All supposed to counter the very effects she was suffering.

Lana stepped out of the tank and wavered under another assault of dizziness. She refused the urge to sit down. She needed to look strong, tough, and ready to go when the other tanks opened. This was her first command. She needed to set out her stall.

One of the tanks had already been vacated for twenty-four hours, as per protocol. The mission's Chief Engineer was required to audit the ship's condition ahead of the crew's *return*.

Returned, not woken.

Stasis was not suspended animation or coma-sleep, it was non-existence. It was oblivion in the truest sense of the word. Stasis was a new technology for humankind, yet another gift from its closest extra-terrestrial ally, the Iaens.

"Commander."

Startled and still a little disorientated, Lana looked round to see the engineer framed in the module's open doorway. Right on time. Kris Andersson, tall, slender and androgynous, their head shaved, their eyes electric blue. And that smile. Lana was a sucker for that smile. Right now, however, they looked as pale and fragile as Lana felt.

"Kris. Good to see you."

"And you Commander."

"Status?" Lana said.

"Out of quantum drive and functioning." Kris's voice was oddly flat, as if the reply was a recitation of what was expected.

Lana saw it then, beneath the calm. She saw it in their eyes and in a hundred other indefinable ways.

"What's wrong Kris? What's happened?"

A moment. Then; "They're all dead."

*

Kris was accustomed to solitude and did not normally equate it with loneliness. The hours spent wandering the ship while the crew drifted through their last remaining hours of post-stasis anaesthesia should have been a treasured moment of peace and contentment. It started out that way, but *this* solitude had become loneliness.

They had returned first, as expected, weak, nauseated, their head battered by the same species of headache to be suffered by their commander when she returned from stasis a few hours later. Kris struggled out of their tank, stood for a moment as the dizziness eased. It took a few seconds for them to understand what they were looking at. There were twenty-four stasis tanks, arranged in two lines across the module. Most of the tanks (they counted twenty) were dark. Kris tried to remember why this was wrong.

There should be a light in each tank, a soft, pearl-hued glow.

So why were twenty of them unlit?

Dead.

Christ. *Dead.*

Kris went to the nearest of them, grabbed at the tank for support and peered in through its transparent lid. Its occupant, Jan van Meyer, according to the nameplate, was out of stasis and should be under anaesthetic sedation. The LEDs on the monitoring panel were off and its vital signs screen was blank. Van Meyer himself was an indistinct shadow in the dark, but Kris could see that there was an unnatural stillness about him. They stabbed the emergency opening pad. The lid slid back with a soft servo-motor whirr.

Kris recoiled, gagging from the smell and the horror that was van Meyer's face.

The man's eyes were wide, and it was as if he was staring into Hell itself. His mouth was locked open in a desperate, silent scream. Suffocation. A nightmare of premature return and waking in a hi-tech coffin, alone, trapped and unable to breathe.

Kris stumbled back, shaking. A moment, to calm down. To push the shock back to where it belonged and regain their professionalism.

Work to do.

Duties.

They re-closed the stasis tank lid. The stench remained and they suspected that it would take many hours for it to be filtered out of the room.

They moved to the three tanks that were still lit and examined their monitors. All functioned perfectly, their occupants in rude health. The nameplates read: Lana Reed, Mission Commander (thank God); Chien Minh, Chief Pilot and Navigator; and Isabella Arias, Chief Communications Officer and Genetic Engineer, responsible for the not-yet-alive passengers in the *Drake's* seed module.

A crew of four, then, who would have to fly a vast

starship the remaining distance to its destination, manoeuvre it into orbit and initiate the seeding of humanity's newest colony. Not impossible, but more likely to end in disaster than triumph.

Kris took a final moment to steady their nerve then set off on their tour of inspection.

The *Drake* was built as a great, vertically-aligned wheel, almost a kilometre in circumference. The rim was divided into a series of modules, joined by link corridors, which gave it the appearance of, in the opinion of some wit back on Earth, a never-ending string of sausages. A transport tube ran around the outside of the rim, through which high speed capsules provided quick access to the various parts of the ship. The two giant sub-light, ion boosters were supported by a tripod structure that projected rearwards from the wheel. The wheel's hub, held in place by a web of metal spokes, contained a microscopic fragment of a black dwarf star. Its massive density provided internal gravity.

The quantum interstellar drive was part of the entire ship, woven, nerve-like into its fabric.

So much of the *Drake*, including the drive, was Iaen technology. Their generosity appeared boundless. There were rumours that they had gifted humanity with immortality, but that the rich and powerful were keeping it for themselves. Kris believed none of it.

The *Drake* felt wrong from the very start of their tour.

There were error messages and alarm records at the first monitoring station they checked. There had been major malfunctions, mostly now repaired or overridden. Temporary fixes were in place to keep the ship on course and functioning until the crew returned.

The next three stations told the same story.

There had been an incident.

An accident.

As they trekked through the eternal downward curve of the ship's corridors, the engineer could glean only hints and clues as to what had happened. It was almost an hour before they noticed the scars that webbed whole sections

4

of wall. The lines were slightly raised and whiter than the light grey finish. Close examination revealed them as evidence of self-repair.

That was another of the Iaens' newly bestowed gifts. Properties had been added to the metalwork of the hull which enabled breaches to heal, provided the damage wasn't catastrophic. Kris wondered what that meant. The sheer amount of scarring indicated that the *Drake* had suffered immense damage. Surely that was catastrophic by anyone's definition.

Their unease turned to fear when they reached the link-corridor that led to the hydroponic farm.

There were scorch marks on the walls. A section of the metalwork was caved in as if punched by a giant fist. At the far end, the farm's bulkhead was blistered and distorted. More self-repair scars were traced over the burned paintwork. Nervous now, Kris palmed the entrance pad.

Entry denied for safety reasons.

"Expand 'safety reasons'."

Farm is irrevocably damaged. Beyond capability of self-repair function.

"Expand 'irrevocably damaged'."

Complete destruction. Insufficient material survived the incident to enable self-repair.

"Define 'incident'."

Possible collision. Auto-logs unable to process data during incident.

This was definitely a catastrophe. The tour of inspection could wait. Kris ran for the nearest transport-capsule and rode it to the command module. The tube was fast, but not fast enough. Kris paced and fretted throughout the eternal three-minute journey.

Possible collision…

Command module. The bridge, the nerve centre, the cockpit. Low curved ceiling. A little cramped. The main vid screen. Four stations: command, comms, navigation and engineering. Each equipped with seat, instrumentation and VR port. The module and all it

contained appeared to be undamaged and fully
functioning. Kris activated the vid-screen. Seventy
percent of the external video feeds were working. Enough
for them to see what was out there.

"Christ," they whispered. "Oh, dear God."

*

The *Drake's* four surviving crew members rode the tube
in silence. Isabella and Chien both appeared to be
suffering from the same post-stasis malaise Lana had
experienced on her own return. She felt for them. They
had not been given as much time as her to recover. Also,
they would have had friends among those who hadn't
made it. They needed to grieve, but that would have to
wait.

Of the three other survivors, Kris was the only one
Lana had worked with on previous missions. Neither she
nor Kris had encountered Chien and Isabella until this
trip. This was – had been – a new crew, assembled for
Lana's first command. They had not been together long
enough to fully bond into a team. So far, however, there
seemed to be no problems between them. Chien,
Vietnamese by birth, was wiry and tough-looking. From
the dealings she had had with him so far, Lana found him
to be professional to his core, quick thinking but not
willing to offer anything of his *self*. Isabella had a
sadness that Lana could not yet pin down. She was
intense, quietly spoken in a way that made her seem ill-
at-ease with other people, but Lana had already come to
trust her and her judgement.

"Okay, Kris, let's have the full status report," Lana
said, as much to break the tense silence in the capsule as
the need for a repeated litany of the problems they faced.

"All necessary systems are functioning," Kris said.
"But there is extensive damage to the hydroponics farm
and most of the upper right quadrant."

"*Extensive* damage?" Chien said.

"Instruments show that there was a collision seventy-three days into the mission."

The crew would have been deep into stasis by then.

"With what?"

"Not known. There's a blank in the auto-logs. The ship probably shut itself down to carry out self-repair after the incident."

"It must have been serious for a shut down like that," Isabella sounded nervous.

"I've yet to run an audit of the *Drake's* memory banks. As far as I can tell, the worst affected section, upper right, was sealed and written-off as beyond repair immediately after the incident, so I haven't been able to get inside. I haven't had a chance to go outside and take a look either. The good news is that life support is working perfectly, but we've probably lost the hydroponic farm. It was close to the impact epicentre."

"We have a stock of pre-packed rations," Chien said. "But without the farm we'll…"

"Eventually starve, unless there's food on Feynman 12," Lana said. "We'll need to address that as a priority. What else Kris?"

"Sorry, commander, I need to show, not tell."

*

"What are we looking at?" Lana's fatigue made her irritable. "Come on, Kris, activate the vid-feed and tell us what the hell is going on."

Kris stood by the screen, which was black and blank. "Commander, the vid feed *is* live." Kris only addressed her as Lana in private. "It's blank because there are no stars."

"What do you mean, no stars?"

"Feynman 12 is within sight of a nebula. It can be seen from the planet's surface at night as a large, glowing cloud that takes up half of its sky in both the north and south hemispheres. If the navigation system is correct, we should be able to see the nebula and surrounding stellar fields in their entirety." Kris waved towards the screen.

"Where are they commander? And where is Feynman's sun?"

"And you're sure the cameras are working," Chien was already at the helm and interrogating the navigation logs.

"All except for Cameras Eight through Twelve. They were probably destroyed in the collision."

"Kris's right." Isabella looked up from the comms panel, headset in place. She sounded shaken. "There's silence out there."

"There's no such thing as silence, even in space," Chien said.

"I am picking up a little noise, black hole signatures, I think, but they're faint. There's nothing else that I can identify. I've never known it to be like this."

"That's impossible." Lana said.

"Listen for yourself, commander." Isabella held out the headset to her.

The challenge, though delivered politely, bordered on the insubordinate but Lana let it go. Everyone was in shock. There would be no tolerance for niceties and protocols.

She took the headset and drew it into place. The silence was immediate and broken only by the gentle roar of her own blood and the barest of static hisses. Stars were loud. They called out into the dark and told their story. Space should be alive with their voices. After a few moments, she returned the set to Isabella and crossed to the screen. She peered into the solid black, willing herself to pick out even the faintest pinpoint of light.

"Navigation error? Could we be in intergalactic space?"

"It would still be noisy" Isabella replied. "Stars shout, galaxies roar."

Kris joined Lana at the screen. The unbroken black held an awful fascination, as if something deep in its heart was calling to them. "Unless we're in some desert so far from everything that we can't hear it."

"Chien, you're certain that there's no sign of Feynman 12?"

Chien didn't reply immediately. He frowned, checked

then re-checked his instruments. Lana waited for him. He was good at what he did. There was obviously a good reason for his hesitation.

"Sorry, commander," he said at last. "I'm plotting our position, using data from the ship's auto-logs. There's a blank. You're right Kris, the ship went into hibernation for a very long…," Chien's voice trailed away. He stared fixedly at his screens and instrumentation. There was a nervous edge to his voice. "Fuck," he said. His distraction dissolved into something that sounded disturbingly like fear. "Commander…No, wait, I'll re-run the data. This can't…"

"What is it?" Lana was unsettled by the pilot's unease. "Chien, talk to me."

"We're not lost," Chien said at last. He sat back, looking even more fragile than he had been on his return. "We're still on course. The collision knocked us off our trajectory, but, according to this, the ship's AI brought us back. We're two AU's from Feynman 12. We should be able to see it as a bright, star-like object, and we should certainly be able to see its sun."

"Instrument damage?" Lana asked.

"Not that I have detected so far," Chien said. "I'm running diagnostics on my station. Test scenarios. Calibration programmes. All positive so far."

Lana took her place in the commander's chair. She had been exhilarated the first time she had taken the station. Now it seemed a lonely place. She felt unprepared. She was a fraud. An imposter.

She closed her eyes and took a breath. Time to line up the challenges. Time to make sense of the swirl of information and impossibilities that obstructed logical thought.

"So, before the quantum drives were engaged, we were hit by some unidentified object, presumably an accident and not an attack. The damage was serious enough –" *Cataclysmic* enough "– for the ship to close-down and execute self-repair." She was afflicted with a sudden vision of the *Drake* spinning out of control, spewing debris, bleeding air and screaming out a cacophony of alarms. Dying while its crew slept the sleep of non-being, unaware and unheeding of the disaster erupting around them. And then twenty of the stasis tanks failed and most of the crew were doomed. The image was terrifying. "There is no record of the timescale for those repairs. Components needed to be re-grown, that can take a long time –"

"Decades," Kris said. "Followed by years of commissioning and test."

"But once the *Drake* was whole again, it resumed its mission, recalculated its course, and returned us from stasis at the correct point in the voyage. Except, it appears that our destination no longer exists."

"Nothing exists," Isabella said.

Lana took a breath. There had to be a logical explanation.

"Chien, run another full diagnostic on your navigation systems. Rip the logs open, find anything that doesn't add up, an uncrossed tee, a full stop where there should be a comma. We have to be somewhere other than where the *Drake* claims we are.

"Isabella, keep listening for every wisp of static. Try to locate the nearest of those black holes. And Kris, I want you to dive into the *Drake's* engineering logs, same as Chien, but first, you and I are going outside."

*

Isabella Arias listened.

She was a musician, her hearing genetically augmented when a child, by parents wealthy enough to ensure that their daughter would be given, what they believed to be, the best start in life. If it meant surgery, implants or modification, so be it, they would DNA-brush the consent form and they would pay whatever it cost.

Isabella was able to tune out her own blood rush. She was able to tune out the rustle of the earphones against her hair and skin. And what she found was blankness. A wall of non-sound. A barrier through which she forced her senses only to find more emptiness.

The silence was black and complete.

Terrifying.

As a child she had often imagined that if she listened hard enough, listened with every iota of her will, she might hear God. She had been convinced that He must speak to His angels, that he must make proclamations to the golden congregation who worshipped Him in the halls of Heaven, and if so, then surely the voice of God would be loud enough for her to hear. But even now, when the universe seemed to have lapsed into silence and when every voice seemed to have been stilled, there was nothing.

That old loneliness was back for the first time since she had left Earth twelve years ago. It had haunted her at the exclusive boarding school she had attended as a child, and in the enormous house that was her home, sun-drenched and light, yet echoing and empty. It had been the core around which she fashioned her determination to gain her parents' approval. Their love was dependent upon her achievements. Success brought praise and gifts. Failure brought coldness and whipcrack rebuke.

On the other hand, the God, preached about and worshipped by Isabella and her parents in the fashionable super-cathedral they attended every Sunday, seemed not to care about achievement and success, a fact that was obviously of no more than lip-service concern to the church's well-heeled congregation. It was, however, vitally important to Isabella. He loved the sinner, the downtrodden, the suffering. She was, it seemed a constant failure and disappointment, regardless of the prizes and awards she brought home from musical competitions for her parent's trophy cabinet. So, surely, God must love her.

Indeed, He became her friend and confidant. As real to her, as the servants who tended to her parents needs and often showed secret kindnesses to her.

The friendship with the Divine was, however, one-sided. He never answered her. She never heard His voice.

Papa and Mama Arias had disowned their daughter the moment she abandoned her music for a career in space. Isabella didn't care. She was glad to escape the coldness and emptiness in which they had buried her. Out here she could commune with the voices that filled this other, far greater emptiness. She was never lonely in space. Starship crews were alive to one another. They relied on you and you on them. They were a rough, fractious family. They were *her* family.

And then there were the stars, who sang to her from the vastness and with whom she could never be lonely.

She also recognised that the barely concealed child part of her hoped, one day, to hear the Voice of God out here. Yes, it was foolish, but she couldn't change or deny what the child felt.

So, she closed her eyes to shut out all other distraction and listened.

The silence crushed her.

"Bella." Chien, his hand on her shoulder.

Startled, Isabella looked up. His expression frightened her.

"I've found something," he said.

His eyes told her that he wished he hadn't.

*

Lana never liked space walks. Since Matt's death, she had travelled the stars, marvelled at the wonders of the Great Out There, risked her life more times than she could remember and worked her way through the ranks until she was given the awful responsibility of command. Climbing into the claustrophobic interior of an EVA suit and stepping from the fragile yet comforting womb of a starship, was another matter altogether. Lana felt as if she was balanced on the lip of a bottomless canyon. This time it was far worse. The hatch had opened to a wall of solid black, so dense it was as if she could reach out and touch it. The airlock lights barely punctured its surface.

A short platform extended out from the threshold of the airlock's outer hatch. To step away from the ship onto the platform seemed an impossible act. As if she was being made to walk the plank by space pirates in some ancient pulp science fiction story. She had no choice, however. She had to go.

"Ready Kris?" she said.

"Ready Commander."

Lana breathed deep and took the step.

Her suit-mounted lamps peeled away the thinnest skin of darkness and revealed nothing. Suddenly the infinite was reduced to a lightless grave only a few metres wide and high. The black was physical, an unthinkable weight of night that bore in from each direction.

She came to herself, grabbed at the rail of the climbing rungs adjacent to the platform, drew the end of her lanyard from its belt-spool and attached it to the stair rail. There was no weightlessness here, which was another oddity. Instead, there was gravity, provided by that minute fragment of incalculably dense white dwarf matter contained in the *Drake's* central hub, many metres beneath her feet. She might not float out here, but she could fall. Hence the lanyard.

Lana took another breath, swung herself round and onto the climbing rungs and ascended to the *Drake's* upper surface. She didn't look down, left, right or upwards but concentrated on the task and on the circle of light thrown against the hull in front of her by her helmet lamp. The solid black infinite assailed her with its vast, limitless, mind-tearing eternity, and crushed her with a formless, dead weight. Claustrophobic as it was, the EVA suit and the closed-in world of its helmet was, this time, a sanctuary from the impossible outside it.

She reached the curved expanse of the upper rim and re-attached the lanyard to the safety rail. A line of guide lights curved away into the dark. The translucent transport tube formed an outer rim to her left and added its own illumination. None of it did more than graze the void's outer skin.

"Kris?"

"Behind you commander."

"I don't like this. I don't like the dark."

"Nor do I."

Lana wanted to reach behind and grab Kris's hand, but that would be yielding to her anxiety, and she needed to fight it.

The glittering energy halo of the now dormant quantum drive came into view. It arched over the *Drake*, some fifty metres out, like a shimmering rainbow in the gloom, but even that did little to alleviate the oppressive, suffocating blackness.

"There's a lot of scarring." Kris's voice crackled into Lana's helmet. "The collision must have been catastrophic."

Lana turned her attention to the metalwork underfoot and for the first time noticed the network of lines that weaved about the various stanchions, scanners and other protrusions that cluttered the *Drake's* hull. The lines did indeed resemble badly healed scars, which was exactly what they were.

Again, Lana felt the terror of a cataclysm she had lived through but not experienced. Unbidden, her imagination reproduced the fiery horror of it, in the same the way it sought to recreate the final moments of her husband's existence as his lander broke apart during a routine descent through the atmosphere of Venus.

"...must have taken years."

"Sorry, Kris? What did you say?" A lapse in concentration. She needed to get herself together.

"I said, the self-repair must have taken years." Kris sounded amused.

Lana glanced out into the dark. It hadn't been wholly successful either. They were not where they were supposed to be, or, more worryingly, where the *Drake* was *telling* them they were.

EVA was exhausting. This EVA more exhausting still because everything was wrong. Lana fought an urge to stare into the blackness. It snagged at her attention more

14

than the graceful bow of the quantum drive. The darkness was total and yet it boiled and writhed and twisted in upon itself as if alive. Things were trying to tear their way through. Unwholesome, awful things –

No, they weren't. There was nothing out there.

A nightmare infinity of *nothing.*

They breasted the curve of the engineering and utilities module to the edge of the smooth valley formed by the corridor between it and the hydroponics farm.

And saw the magnitude of the disaster.

There was an immense hole in the farm's hull, as if the metalwork had been smashed open by a giant fist. The hole was at least five metres in width, and even wider in places. The metal around the wound was blackened and heat-seared, the edges contorted into great bubbles and folds, like the solidified lava fields Lana had seen in Iceland, back on Earth.

A vacation with Matt, their last before his final voyage.

Lana crossed to the hole and peered down into the ship. All the lighting had failed. There was only a darkness every bit as deep as the night out here.

"I'm going in," she said.

"I should go first, commander."

"Overruled."

Lana clipped her lanyard to the stanchion of a nearby sensor tower. The top of the tower had been torn away, but its base seemed solid enough. She activated the spool's drive then manoeuvred herself through the wound, careful not to tear the suit on its jagged, scorched edges, and dropped into the cavernous interior of the hydroponics farm. The spool vibrated through her suit as it played out the line.

It was like a descent into a night-black ocean. Dust swirled through the beam of Lana's suit lamp. She became aware that Kris had joined her when the beam of their helmet lamp crossed hers. The combined lights revealed that they were about twenty metres from the floor.

Nothing remained whole or undamaged. Severed pipes

and cables hung about them like the roots of giant trees. They stopped their descent at three metres above the floor. It was too dangerous to continue. Their lamps revealed a wasteland, made ghostly by the stark beams of light. The rows of troughs that had once contained the soil and plants were nothing but a mountain range of twisted metal. The soil was frozen white. Whatever had been growing there was now dust, organic tissue torn to pieces by ice. The irrigation system hung above the devastation, a lethal spider web of broken and tangled pipes, and support wires. Everything metal was scorched black, burned by the energy released during the collision.

"There's been no attempt at self-repair here," Kris said.

"A decision to save the rest of the ship at the expense of this section?"

"Possible. The ship's AI might've assumed that the pre-packs would give us enough time to solve the food problem, or that we would find a food source on Feynman 12."

"Except Feynman 12's not out there."

There's nothing *out there*.

Lana experienced a momentary dread. They couldn't fully trust the *Drake* anymore. They didn't know where they were, and it was likely that they were going to starve.

"Commander." Chien's voice startled her.

"Reed here."

"Commander, you need to get back to the control module." The pilot sounded badly shaken. "Bella and I have found something, in the navigation logs. You need to see this."

Lana and Kris activated the lanyard spools and swept back up through the tangles of broken pipes, ducts and severed cables. They worked together, back-to-back and slowly rotating as they ascended, warning one another to dodge and jink to avoid collision; broken limbs were bad enough, torn suits would mean almost instant asphyxiation. It was slow and exhausting work.

Astonished that they were still intact, Lana and Kris

emerged from the great wound in the *Drake's* hull and began the arduous trek back to the airlock. It was then, following the guide lights through the industrial landscape that grew from the ship's outer skin, that Lana's unease turned to raw fear.

The darkness was terrifying.

The totality of it.

The eternity of it.

The utter and complete nothingness that demanded her comprehension then threatened to break her mind as it grappled with the concept.

It isn't empty, her sub-conscious whispered. Everything you dread, every sin and mistake you have ever made is out there.

Matt is out there.

You fought, didn't you, the darkness said, on the evening before he left for his last trip. There in the married quarters at the star port. What did you expect, Lana? Forgiveness? Did you really believe that a tearful confession would open his arms and that he would shower you with kisses as he told you that everything was all right?

You fucked another man. You betrayed Matt. It doesn't matter how lonely you were that night, or how drunk. You took what you and Matt held precious and gave it to a loud, drunken nonentity whose name you can't even remember. It meant nothing to you until you woke the next morning, alone in that hotel room, sober enough for guilt and regrets. To Matt, on the other hand, it meant a trampled heart and broken promises.

It meant preoccupation and a momentary lapse of concentration...

Christ, Lana, you weren't even unhappy with Matt. In fact, you loved him so much it hurt. So why? Moment of weakness? Too many G-and-T's? Greed? Lust? The loneliness of the spacefarer's wife? Come on, you were a senior ground crew technician. You knew the score when you married him. Which cliché fits, Lana? Which excuse?

The fight was terrible. Love turned to hate. Sweetness to bitterness. Desire to poison.

Twenty-seven hours later, Lana was a widow.

Seventeen months after that, she entered flight training, graduated and seldom set foot on Earth again. In three years, she was given command of the *Drake* for a deep-space, colony seeding mission. She needed this voyage. She needed to be a long way from Earth. She needed to run and hide.

Except there was no hiding, because it was all there, swirling through the darkness like a black clot of liquid guilt.

*

"Okay, what've you found?" Lana was back in the control module, putting on a brusque and professional act to cover her anxiety. The *Drake* was seriously damaged. Their food stocks finite. They were lost. Yet, she had to remain commander; cool, calm and collected.

There were problems to solve.

Chien glanced at Isabella. She nodded. The signal for him to speak.

"Okay," he said. "The quantum drive works on the entanglement principle, yes?"

"It does," Kris said.

"The simultaneous existence of identical particles in different locations in space. The drive does this artificially, recreating the necessary particles in the vicinity of a mission destination. The originals are discarded, and the new ones activated."

Always an awful concept to Lana, because discarded meant obliterated. How many times had she been annihilated and re-born, memories and personality intact?

Sins un-atoned for?

"Basic, but essentially correct," Kris said.

"We had to dig deep," Chien seemed irritated by Kris's response. "But the data seems to show that the drive is not only able to create entangled particles in space, but also in time."

"In time?" Lana said. "Are you saying that we've travelled through time?"

"That isn't possible," Kris said. "There's no evidence that it can be done. There are too many paradoxes, too many variables. And time isn't real. It *is* and then *isn't*. The past and future don't exist."

"Let him finish, Kris."

"Thank you, commander." Chien resumed his explanation. "I've torn the logs apart, as you requested and hunted down the entanglement code. I found a discrepancy between the programmed code and the one instigated by the ship. The damage to the *Drake* was much worse than we thought. The guidance system and quantum location array were affected, and the original code corrupted."

"Not so much that it couldn't instigate a jump," Kris said.

"True. We, that's Bella and I –"

Bella and I? Something had happened between those two. Lana wasn't surprised, there had been an obvious attraction the moment the selected crew first met.

" – think that the *Drake* managed to reconstruct the code as it believed it should be, but it made errors."

"As if it was suffering from concussion and was memory-impaired," Kris said.

"The *Drake* isn't a living organism."

"It was analogy, Chien. Although I wouldn't be so sure about the living part."

"And this man is supposed to be an engineer." Chien's low-level irritation had transformed into sarcasm. "God help us."

Lana knew immediately that the male personal pronoun was no slip of the tongue. There was a different kind of tension between the pilot and engineer. Lana could tell that Chien had little time for those he saw as fools. *She* found him intimidating and although he tended to obey orders, she could feel his disapproval for those he considered to be bad ones. But this outburst was completely out of character. It was childish and petty.

"Fuck you, Chien –"

"Enough, both of you," Lana said. "Chien, apologise. Now."

"We have bigger problems than Kris Andersson's hurt feelings."

No matter how deeply Lana was concerned about Kris's feelings, she knew that Chien was right, but there could be no survival if the crew fell apart.

Kris was on their feet, fists clenched. "What the hell have you got against me, Chien?"

"Are you telling me that you really don't know, Andersson?"

"No, I don't."

"Hoyle."

Kris blanched. "Hoyle? What has that to do with you and me?"

Lana pushed between them and found herself face-to-face with the pilot, a signal that she sided with Kris. She turned away, arms out, Chien on her right, Kris on her left. "You both need to calm down, and you need to apologise, Chien."

"Fuck that."

"It's not a request." Lana knew that this was no longer about an argument over the ship's possible sentience. This was about her authority.

Still Chien didn't comply. Lana had no idea of her next move in this game. The ship had a holding cell. Spacers sometimes broke under the madness of what they were expected to do, by the isolation and sheer impossibility of the universe. Surely Chien's reluctance to back down didn't warrant incarceration.

"Chien. Apologise. That is an order."

"Chi." Isabella, suddenly on her feet, hand on the pilot's arm, her voice gentle, placating. "Kris deserves an apology. We can't fight among ourselves. Please, Chi."

The pilot looked at her, nodded then sighed and muttered something that might have been "Sorry."

Relieved and grateful for Isabella's intervention, Lana said, "All right, let's calm down and take a breath. I understand, this is too big to handle easily. Isabella's right. Fighting each other will be the end of us."

This is the end of us…

"Chien, have you been able to establish our position?" Lana said.

"We are *where* we are supposed to be," Chien said. "But not *when*."

"What are you trying to tell me?"

"The quantum jump was temporal. It took us forwards, into the future. A long way into the future."

"How far?"

"Over to you Bella."

"We're not sure, exactly, the logs are corrupted," Isabella said. "But I believe that we are at a point long after the universe has gone dark."

"What brings you to that conclusion?"

"I've finally managed to pick up some very weak stella radio emissions as well as signals from black holes. The star talk is weak because they are signals that have been travelling for a long time and from a long way off, I mean, an unimaginable distance away, which means that they are echoes. The stars themselves are probably long gone. There are no signals strong enough to be from anything close." She waved towards the screen. "And there is no light, nothing. The light sensors are picking up no photons whatsoever, not even the barest of featherlight touches."

"What does that mean?" Lana knew what it meant. Kris and Chien both knew, but she wanted Isabella to say it. She wanted Isabella to state the impossible.

And she did. "All the stars have died. The lights have been out for millennia. We are deep into the darkness

"But that's a jump of billions of years."

"Trillions, for the universe to be this quiet."

*

"We have to find a way back." Lana was not certain that the statement hadn't emerged as a plea. For a moment it felt like a cry for help from inside a buried coffin. No one could hear. No one would come to their aid because there was no one.

Christ, no one.

No light. No heat.

No life.

Except for the four humans huddled in their metal wheel, struggling to stay sane in the face of such an awful truth and wrestling with the knowledge that their resources were limited. No matter how much of their water, waste and atmosphere was recycled by the ship's life support systems, how much electrical power was generated by the Drake's radiative cold sky power station, technology failures, hunger and plain old entropy would eventually silence the ship and its crew. Their only decision then would be whether to end their lonely suffering quickly or hold on to hope until their last agonised breath.

Lana noted that the others looked pale and drawn, obviously battling their own terrors. To get home required passage across an incomprehensible gulf of time, a near infinite ocean.

Okay, activity and purpose. They were not finished yet.

"Kris, you need to work with Chien, locate the fault, the point at which it all went wrong. Pinpoint the nature of the fault itself. It's there somewhere, in the logs. You need to be forensic in your approach. Take another look at the collision site. There will be residue, particles of whatever struck the ship. Read everything we have on quantum drive technology and research. This can be reversed.

"Isabella, keep listening. Let me know the moment you hear anything. *Anything*, okay?"

"Yes, commander."

"This is a lot to ask of you all. Rest when you need to. That's an order. I'll organise the rations and see what I can do about setting up some sort of replacement farm. We have a stock of seeds and soil in the colony-starter modules. I'm also going to take a look at the protos." The

22

other seeds they carried. "I'll need you for that, Isabella. In an hour?"

"Yes, commander."

"I'm also aware that we haven't grieved for those who died. Twenty of our fellow crew are gone. We are probably the last humans in existence, but we *are* in existence. We are human. We need to continue for as long as we are able. While we are alive and fighting to survive there is a human race in this universe. And part of being human and alive is to give our dead the respect and honour they deserve. So, we'll hold a funeral, this time tomorrow. Agreed?"

Agreed.

*

"What did Chien mean by *Hoyle*?"

They lay together in Lana's bunk, Kris on their back, Lana's head resting on their chest. Lana was warmed by their lovemaking, in the soft glow and contentment it brought. Kris was gentle with her, almost languid. Those moments were when time stopped, and she fell into blissful non-thought. But now, as it always had to, the afterglow was fading.

"I don't want to talk about it." Kris drew away from her and sat up.

"Hey, it's okay. I'm sorry."

"So am I." Kris had their arms about their knees. "It was bad, that's all. But it's done."

"Chien doesn't think so."

"Well Chien can go to Hell."

"No, Kris, he can't." Lana was up beside them now. "We have to stay together as a crew. We can't afford to break up over some argument or slight or whatever this is."

"I don't know what it is."

"Then you should confront him and ask."

"No, if he has a problem with me then it's up to him to tell me what it is."

23

"You're too bloody stubborn for your own good, Kris. This is going to fester. It has to be resolved."

Kris didn't speak or move but remained hunched about themself. Whatever had happened on Hoyle, it had been terrible.

"I could order you," she said.

"Then order me."

Lana sighed. "No, I won't but, please Kris, talk to him. Heal this."

"Okay, okay. I'll talk to Chien when I'm ready."

"Thank you. I need him, and I need you. Christ, I need you."

*

Chien was outside. Protocol demanded that there be a minimum of two people on any EVA, but, surely, protocol meant less and less in their current predicament. Chien trudged across the upper hull towards the hydroponics module, ostensibly to look for fragments of whatever had hit the *Drake*, but also because he needed time away from the others, even Bella, for whom he felt something that might be the beginnings of love.

He had noticed her straightaway during the *Drake's* first crew muster back on Earth. She struck him as lonely, not good at mingling with a crowd. She had stood on the periphery and watched him, and Chien felt something resembling an electric shock each time he caught her eye. She was serious, dedicated, not given to distraction and small talk. He could tell. Because she was like him.

Relationships between crew members were discouraged.

But surely that didn't matter anymore and even if it did, Chien didn't care because it was increasingly obvious that Lana and Andersson spent time alone together and were making little effort to conceal it. When he had finished out here, Chien was going to talk to Isabella and tell her how he felt. It would not be easy. Talking from the heart and not the head was never something Chien Minh relished.

He was also worried about Lana. It was clear to Chien that she was too fragile to lead this crew through their current crisis. She would break, eventually. Chien was sure of it, and it terrified him.

As for Kris Andersson. He...they...might be a good engineer.

But Chien had discovered that they were also a coward.

His search through the logs had taken him into the crew profile database. Curious, and acutely aware that he needed to rely on the three other survivors to stay alive, he opened their files, starting with Andersson's. And there, like a knife to the guts, was a citation for bravery. Admirable, except that Kris Andersson had been the lander pilot during the Hoyle rescue mission.

Of all the space farers, Chien could have ended up with here in the dark universe, he was shoulder-to-shoulder with the person who had killed his sister. He had almost broken down under the weight of his re-opened grief and rage that moment, there in the command module, but he had held it back. He had remained silent. He had closed the file and returned to the work Lana had set for him, until that flare-up a few hours ago. That was a foolish mistake. He had allowed his gut to overrule his sense.

Chien knew that he needed to keep his new and sudden hatred of the androgyne in check. He had worked hard for his position. He had overcome personal tragedy and trauma by sheer force of will. He had crushed the horrors of his past deep into his sub-conscious where they belonged and dedicated himself to his career. He would not fail now or throw it way for the sake of a wretch like Andersson.

There was a third reason why Chien was outside. The iron cell that imprisoned his past had fractured. The monsters were clawing for release and had driven him out here to see and feel the darkness for himself.

He needed to know it.

He stopped walking and turned to stare into its face.

For him, there was no vastness to it, no sense of distance. It felt as though its face was up against his own. His helmet lamp pushed a beam into the dark, but it revealed nothing and was swallowed only a few metres out.

Chien knew the dark. He had spent many childhood nights hiding in the jungles of Vietnam and Cambodia, looking out for himself and Nyung, his younger sister. That jungle darkness had not been as silent as this one. Jungles are never quiet. But the fear was the same. The fear that someone or something was coming for him, for Nyung and for the huddled, rag tag collection of refugees of which they were part.

There were countless enemies back then. South-East Asia had been devastated by apocalyptic storms that had drowned its coasts and hurled the sea kilometres inland. Law and order quickly dissolved to be replaced by militia, bandits and terrorists. There was no one to trust and no sanctuary. Even refugee groups would turn on one another if they crossed paths in the jungles or the highlands. Everyone bribed, fought, raped, extorted, and destroyed. There was no government, no structure, only the inexorable urge to head west to the near-mythical UN camps where there was a rumour of warmth and safety.

Disease, raids, poisonous snakes and storms took more than half of Chien's group. He was fourteen, Nyung eleven, the last survivors of a family drowned by the floods. Alone, they had taken to the lethal streets of Hanoi and learned early how to make a little money and stay alive. It took a year of degradation and petty crime to raise the extortionate fare to join a refugee group.

If the city was Hell, the jungle was its ninth circle. At night, Chien would stand and defy its blackness until he collapsed from exhaustion. Nothing would get to his sister without having to go through him first. If the moment came, he would die on his own terms and that was somehow less terrifying than having his throat slit while he slept.

He had protected Nyung and brought her out of those jungles alive.

He had not been able to protect her years later, when she travelled to Hoyle.

Andersson was supposed to protect her then, but they ran.

And she died.

This dark, however, was not to be defied and after a few moments, Chien could bear it no longer. He turned away and resumed his trek to the hydroponics module.

The hole was shockingly big and brutal. A vast black wound in the flesh of the ship. Chien moved closer and noted that the torn, molten-then-frozen edges curved downwards. The rippling indicated a sudden, explosive burst of heat. Although it was difficult to make out detail in the light of the guide lamps and the limited disc of illumination from his helmet and suit lamps, he could see scorch marks radiating from the crater.

He moved closer then knelt and began scraping up flakes of the burned paint. Nearer to the hull itself he found fragments, melted into the metal. He opened his tool kit looking for an extractor. He would need to heat and soften the area around the fragment to loosen them and prise them out. It was going to take a while.

Out here.

In the utter loneliness of a dead universe.

*

The seed module was a separate vessel, fitted into the rim diametrically opposite to the control module. The nose which contained the module's flight control station was slotted neatly into the link between it and one of the storage modules. Its tail and drive tubes, into the link that joined it to the recreation module.

The seeder's main body was a vast cylinder, lined with womb pods. A multi-storey central gantry provided a main access route, from which others led away to a complex of inspection platforms that ran along the sides of wombs themselves.

Virtually all the pods glowed with the soft inner light that denoted healthy occupants. Isabella and Lana walked along opposing gantries, checking the monitor pads for each section of one hundred wombs. The contents of each womb was obscured by dense, ochre-hued fluid. There wouldn't have been much to see anyway, the occupants were shapeless conglomerations of cells. They were blanks, ready to be moulded into whatever variation of human being was needed for survival on their new home planet.

That was Isabella's other responsibility. As genetic engineer, she was the potter who would shape the clay.

Except that it seemed unlikely that these proto-humans would ever be required, because no stars meant no planets. They were doomed to die, unborn, heedless of their fate.

The sight of these serried ranks of genetic blanks disturbed Lana. She had been in here before, of course, but now it had the smell of slave-ship about it. The protos were not suffering. They had no awareness, but they were the stuff of human beings and had been crowded into the hold of a ship. Their destiny was to work for humankind and build another world for them to claim and exploit.

Lately, it seemed to Lana that her species had degenerated into a crowing, prideful mob. They had rejected the friendship of others and thrown in their lot with the Iaens, whom many seemed to see as gods and all-but worshiped. Especially since it had been revealed that, although they usually presented themselves in a rough-hewn humanoid form, they were, in fact, bodiless collectives of energy and id. Purely spiritual, like angels. Like God Himself.

Humankind clamoured for unfettered expansion, new worlds and plundered resources.

Lebensraum.

Conquest.

Of course, no one used the c-word, but in Lana's view, that was what it was. This ship, its cargo and purpose as a colony seeder, were, if she was brutally honest, emblems of that greed. No sentient life on Feynman 12, the mission's destination? That was the conclusion of the pathfinder team who had visited it five years previously –

five trillion years previously. But who the hell was any human being to judge where sentience began or what form it took? Not all intelligent life was carbon-based. Humankind had encountered all manner of impossible manifestations of sentience since the Iaens helped it become star-borne, and yet the old prejudices remained.

Despite her misgivings, Lana was here, on this ship, because space was her home now. There was nothing left for her on Earth. This was the only place she was at peace. To get into space required compromise. Also, the final decision as to whether the planet could be colonised was hers. She had promised herself that she would explore all avenues of possible native sentience before giving the go-ahead. Thus was her conscience eased.

But not salved.

She met up with Isabella at the far end of the module, by the hatch to its flight command station.

"All okay?"

"Three failures."

"I found six." Well within the acceptable limits. Lana leaned over the gantry rail. From there she had a view of the module and its ranks of womb tanks. "Not that it matters. We're never going to birth them."

"There's always hope," Isabella said. "We might find an orphan planet, a star, somewhere we can land and set up a colony."

"I admire your optimism."

"The universe might have gone dark, but for these people," she waved toward the tanks, "it will be their home. I will mould them to live in the dark and cold if necessary. Life is…life. It deserves to have its chance. Someone said that the universe only exists when there are people there to experience it."

"'Consciousness is the phenomenon by which the universe's existence is made known.' Roger Penrose the mathematician. You make a good point, Isabella, but, realistically, what are the chances of finding anything to land on?"

"Impossibly low."

"Low isn't zero. I'll take low."

"Me too." Isabella said. "If we find a world, we can create something good. We can give humankind a second chance." She meant it. Her optimism was refreshing.

Lana placed a hand on Isabella's shoulder. "Get some rest. If there's something out there trying to get our attention, it'll still be there in eight hours' time.

*

Chien stood outside Isabella's quarters. He was nervous and noticed that his hand trembled as he made to activate the intercom pad. He hesitated, appalled at his reticence but also bemused that he could stand and face a darkness filled with all manner of death and yet was afraid to speak to Isabella over the intercom.

"Yes? Who is there?"

"Chien. Bella, I need to talk to you."

The door opened to reveal Isabella Arias. She wore a plain robe. Her dark hair was down and loose about her face and shoulders. She looked uncertain. Afraid even.

Chien tried to frame a sentence. "Bella…I…"

She came to him, put her arms about him and kissed him and for a moment there was no more darkness.

*

The stasis tanks would have to be their graves. The task of removing the bodies of the twenty crew who had not survived was, in Lana's opinion, too awful a task, both physically and emotionally, for the four survivors to undertake. Instead, the climax of the short, simple ceremony would be to return the dead to stasis, which was as near to oblivion as was possible.

To do this, the tanks needed to work.

Leaving Isabella to continue her aural search of the universe in which they had found themselves and Kris to concentrate on the engineering logs and co-operate with Chien in finding a way out of this predicament, Lana took it upon herself to attempt a repair to the tanks. However, being here, alone, in the deep space travel module, was not something she relished.

It was brightly lit. There were no shadowed corners, and the bodies were hidden from view in their high-tech coffins. There was nothing to fear. Nothing to cause unease. She had a technical problem to solve and solve it she would.

And yet, she was frightened.

Not uneasy or nervous.

She was afraid.

It had begun when she exited the transport tube and set off down the corridor for the final walk to the module. It was dread. It was the silence. It was the night that pushed in at the walls of the ship. It was the echo of her own footsteps. She fought it, tried to dismiss it as ridiculous, as weakness, as a foolishness she needed to overcome before it consumed her and made her useless.

When the module hatch slid open and she stepped inside, that dread became fear.

Lana stood and gazed over the darkened, closed-down tanks. Each contained a badly decomposed corpse. The dead, who could do her no harm, who would never move or speak again. She was here to carry out tests on the electrical supply, on the stasis processor itself. She was here to carry out engineering tasks, not to hold a séance or rob graves.

She crossed to the main control panel, unlocked its lid and set to work.

Lana.

Matt?

No, he was dead. And definitely not here. He didn't even leave a corpse, only debris and fragments of organic material scattered over the surface of Venus and blasted into space.

Don't ignore me.

Didn't you hear me? There was nothing left of you, Matt.

Lana stared hard at the tester as she worked

methodically through each circuit. She ignored the voice because there *was* no voice. She didn't look round. Despite his presence. Despite the need to see him.

Twenty circuits. No faults. Puzzled, Lana logged in to the stasis processor itself and downloaded its logs. God they were slow. She wanted to be done, and out of here.

Lana, Lana, don't ignore me, bitch.

Not him. Matt never spoke to her like that. Whoever you are, you are not him.

Whoa, what the hell was she doing? Talking back to the voices in her own head? Really?

Data, that was what was important, not her own fevered imagination. Hard cold data. Fact. Reality.

Lana. Please.

No. I'm not playing, okay?

Something flickered in the walls, glimpsed in the periphery of her vision. Ghosts?

Of course not. She peered at the text on the processor's screen. *System failure, tanks five through twenty-four.* No reason given, no explanation.

Current status?

Functional.

Lana, please. Lana you betrayed me, please at least look me in the eye and tell me you still love me.

Functional? So why did the tanks shut down?

System failure, tanks five through twenty-four.

She knew that.

Why? Not what, why for Christ sake?

System failure, tanks five through twenty-four. That's what it was, Lana. That's all you need to know –

Shut up.

– because you can't be trusted, can you? You bitch. I thought I could trust you, but you betrayed me.

Shut up.

Betrayed us. Didn't you Lana, didn't you. You betrayed us, you can't be trusted…

And all the while those shapes cavorted through the walls, never fully seen, never still; figures, monstrous forms, clouds. The incessant flicker made her sick and faint. Lana could no longer think. She trembled too violently to re-set the tanks. She wanted to run. She wanted to scream at the voice to –

"Shut up!"

Startled by the sound, she froze then willed herself to calm down. Willed the voice into silence. Willed herself not to turn round.

Lana.

No –

The beat of a fist against a tank lid almost took her legs from under her. Lana stumbled back and spun about. The lights failed then pulsed back into life, their stroboscopic madness in sync with the pounding.

Then there were more, an eruption of desperate hammer blows from inside every tank.

Let us out. For God's sake let us out.

Figures danced over the walls, shadows that beat at its surface from within the wall fabric.

We can't breathe…We're suffocating…Lana, in the name of Christ let us out…

She clamped her hands over her ears and lurched towards the hatch. She had to pass between the tanks. She had to let them out or they would die.

Thud thud thudthud thudthudthud –

It hurt her head. It consumed her. It wouldn't end.

"Stop it. *Stop* it!"

Silence, but for the gentle hiss and thrum of the *Drake's* life sounds. The light was steady and bright. The tanks dark. Lana returned her attention to the control panel. She waited for her breathing to slow and the shaking to ease then activated the tanks. The light came on in each one. Their monitoring panels came to life.

The processor screen pronounced them as fully functional. There was no technical reason for their occupants to have died. Their deaths appeared to have been the result of a decision made by the ship's AI to shut down their tanks.

System failure, tanks five through twenty-four.

The *Drake* had murdered them. Or it had been

programmed to do so. Impossible, of course, but what other explanation could there be?

Lana decided to keep it from the crew for now.

She switched off the tanks. The next time they were activated would be at the funeral.

*

The next day, at the appointed time, Kris, Chien and Isabella filed in and took their places in a tight little arc about their mission commander. Lana had returned to the deep space travel module early. She needed to face down the madness she had found in here yesterday. So far, the stasis tanks had been silent, their occupants at rest. There were no voices.

The others all looked strained and tired, despite rigorously enforced rest periods. Lana doubted that she looked to be any healthier. Sleep had eluded her, driven out by a grim meld of hopelessness and guilt.

"We're here to pay our respects to our crewmates who have given their lives in service to humankind." Dry and pompous, but she didn't know what else to say. "They all knew that the spacefarer's life is a dangerous and precarious one. They all knew the risks and yet, stepped up to take their places in the first rank." Lana found herself becoming surprisingly emotional. "We may have friends among them. We may not have known any of them well. We were a new crew assembled for this mission, but they are our kin. I suggest we pause for a moment to pay them some private honour."

She glanced at Kris. The engineer stood on Isabella's left, head bowed, trembling slightly.

Something was wrong with what she saw.

Lana needed Kris at that moment, and it looked as if they needed her just as badly.

"Okay," Lana said. "Does anyone want to say anything?"

No one did, so, relieved that she could get this over with, she laid her palm on the control pad of the nearest of the stasis tanks and said a quiet "Bon voyage". The others moved among the rest of the tanks and did the same. Each was lit briefly, then went dark.

Lana watched them, uneasy now. Something was wrong with this. Something out of kilter that went beyond the obvious wrongness of the situation. Something that lodged in her mind like a splinter.

*

The *Drake* hung in space. It was a ring of light in utter blackness. It had no destination.

Being human, the crew convinced themselves that it was their duty to find ways to prolong their existence. The only real task that carried any meaning at all was the search for a way back to their own time. Days passed, a week, two weeks, then three, marked, not by the rise and set of any sun or the steady cycle of light and dark, but by the pure mathematics of the *Drake's* chronometer.

Three weeks of lonely monotony, and of routine that provided structure and purpose for the crew's lives. They occasionally swapped duties; both to alleviate the boredom and in the belief that a fresh eye or ear might result in some breakthrough.

And all the time, the crew's will was steadily, inexorably eroded by fading hope, the vast silent emptiness of the ship, the infinite darkness outside its walls, and by the demons that darkness had freed from the confines of their psyche.

For Lana, it was guilt.

For Kris, it was their father's contempt and the apocalyptic horror of Hoyle.

For Chien, it was the darkness and what it hid.

*

For Isabella, it was the silence.

Once more at her station, lost in the void, she heard nothing that could be a star or even a planet. But she was sure she could hear a voice, one that spoke to her and only her. She told no one else. Not even Chien.

Her lover.

She had never been this happy. He fulfilled her. He completed her. When he had appeared at her door and they kissed, when they stumbled, entwined and grabbing at each other, it felt as if every thread of her life had been woven into the tapestry of that moment.

He was a hard man, tough, taciturn, damaged by the horrors he had experienced as a youth. Isabella did not attempt to force her way into that pain. He would tell her when he was ready. She was sure of that. But those horrors emerged from the depths of his subconscious when he was asleep beside her. They signalled to her in restlessness and broken phrases that told of darkness, pursuit, and the death of those he loved.

She could do no more than hold him and murmur comforts. Chien was the anchor, the meaning. He was kind to her and gentle with her. When she was with him, she did not have to think about the darkness outside and whatever spoke to her from its depths.

But even the joy of new-found love could not quench her need of the voice.

It was a drug to her, the desire to listen and hear that soft whisper drift out of the darkness. When it did, she experienced a moment of euphoria, but it always faded as quickly as it came. A part of her knew that she was obsessed, and that any imagined, whisper-like sound was interpreted by her sub-conscious as a voice. She knew that the good feeling it brought was simply a dopamine hit, stimulated by the hope that they were not alone out here.

"Bella?" Chien, on the commer.

"Chi?"

"I'm in the lab. I've found something. It's not good. Please come here. I need you."

*

Lana always found physical labour to be therapeutic which was why she was in the maintenance workshop. Not required in the command module, she had set about the task of rigging up some way to grow food. She had found a stack of large plastic ducts, taken them to the machine shop, sliced them into makeshift troughs, and drilled small drainage holes into their undersides. Crude but effective.

Job done, she decided to take a walk to the colony stores and find soil and seeds.

The noise of power tools had only drowned out the clamorous inner voices for a short while.

When she walked, there was silence.

The corridor curved monotonously downwards into the distance, bordered by arched grey-white walls, lined with pipes and ductwork and lit by an endless series of LED plates. The hull's inner surface was, for several metres at a time, smooth then, suddenly, webbed with self-repair scarring. Lana's footsteps echoed back from the walls.

Melded with others.

She stopped.

Other footsteps? No, there were no other footsteps. It was echoes. It was her own tiredness and imagination. There was no one else. The ship was mostly empty.

Utterly empty.

She resumed walking.

The footsteps were back.

"Kris? Is that you? Chien? Isabella?"

No answer. Nor should there be.

"Kris?"

There was someone ahead of her, just below the shoulder of the everlasting curve. She made to call out again but stopped herself. She didn't want to know who it was.

Because there was no one there.

Are you sure, Lana?

No. If there really was someone there it could only be a fifth crew member who had survived and was now wandering the ship lost and disorientated.

There was no fifth crew member. There were only four survivors.

She was suddenly convinced that whoever walked ahead of her, had stopped, and was waiting.

He was waiting.

"Matt?" The name was out before she could prevent it. "Matt, is that you?"

God, it was him. She broke into a run, desperate to reach him before he resumed his walk. Over the curve, on and on.

"Matt. *Matt.*"

There. Him. Tall, broad, every inch the space hero, ambling in that easy, oddly graceful walk of his. He had his back to her. Wearing civvies, a tee shirt and jeans. The clothes he had been wearing on the night of their last fight.

Lana pushed herself into a final sprint.

Then he ran. He didn't look back. Lana couldn't bear it.

"Please look at me. Matt. Please –"

She stumbled to a halt. The corridor was empty. Lana was bereft. She began to cry. She murmured his name over and over and slumped against the curved, grey-white wall. She felt the rough landscape of its scars. She didn't care. She wanted Matt. She wanted to hold him and bury herself in him and tell him that she was sorry.

He was gone. He had never been here. Matt was dead.

She needed Kris.

She needed them to consume her in that quiet, complete way of theirs. She needed to lose herself and fade into the beautiful oblivion they offered. Kris was a *presence* during those moments, vast, powerful and glorious. The many sides of their essence surrounded her and held and caressed and took her and it was good.

No, she had to find her own way out of this self-created darkness. She was losing control of the mission and could never restore it by running and hiding from monsters the moment she left her ready room.

There was a war to win. And today was the day.

"I am the mission commander," she said, out loud.

Really? said Matt, the voice of the infinite nothing, the jester inside her own head.

"Fuck you."

Lana stepped out into the corridor and set off in the direction of the command module.

Come on, where are you?

She fought the urge to glance over her shoulder. Even when her footsteps mingled with other footfalls. She felt him behind her. His presence strong and certain. His stare bore into the back of her neck. She heard his breath. She heard her name. She refused to turn. She refused to believe.

Lana.

Walk. Fucking *walk*.

You betrayed me. You spat on our love.

She spun round. "Yes, Matt. But it's too late to do anything about it. You're dead. You're gone."

Nothing, but the long ever-descending curve of the corridor. Nothing but its endless highway of identical lights and curved, grey-white walls.

She started to laugh then but stopped her mirth dead. That laughter hadn't felt healthy, or controllable.

She walked.

Lana...

Show yourself. Come on. Where are you?

The challenge was defiant, but it also terrified her.

Lana, don't...

Where are you? You're not here. This is my ship.

Is it?

This is my fucking ship.

It's not, Lana.

Matt. In the shadows, coming for her. Out there in the cold, endless nothing.

In her head.

They don't trust you, Lana. I don't trust you.

They trust me. They're a good crew. They're professional.

They're alone and adrift. They don't have an anchor because you've broken free and left them to die.

No, I haven't. I'm trying to keep them alive. I'm going to save them.

You faithless bitch. Alone and adrift and drunk and ripe for the picking, weren't you. Oh, you poor lonely little space widow. Husband away fulfilling his destiny. You left behind. Earthbound. Lonely, lonely, lonely –

"All right, all right, for God's sake, I'm sorry."

Her voice was shocking in the silence.

She walked on.

She would not be afraid.

This was her ship. She was its commander. It was dead matter. It was empty. There was nothing here.

She reached a badly damaged section. The walls and the floor were laced with self-repair scars. The electrical systems were riddled with faults. The monitoring panels blinked warning and alarm messages. It was cold here. The heating units unreliable. Nothing life-threatening but in need of repair.

There was someone waiting up ahead. Glimpsed then gone, then back. He was trying to catch her out. He didn't trust her. Well, perhaps he was right not to, but it was only once so why couldn't he understand that?

He didn't want to, that was why.

"It was a mistake. I'm sorry. I'm so fucking sorry, okay?"

She stopped. There was nothing. There was no one else. She was talking to herself. She needed to stop.

Lana, Lana, listen to me. Lana.

Go away, Matt. I don't want to talk to you. I don't want to see you. I've told you everything.

You broke my heart, so I killed myself and my crew.

No, you didn't. It was an accident. You hit the atmosphere at too acute an angle. The lander dissolved in the heat.

I burned, Lana. I burned because of you. My crew died because of you. It was your fault. You drove me to it.

No.

Yes.

His fist slammed into the hull, from outside.

Outside?

Again.

Deafening this time.

40

Lana. Lana. Lana. Lana. Commander CommanderCommanderLanaCommanderlana...

Lana pressed her hands over her ears but the pounding went on and on.

She stumbled back and the scarred metal of the hull bent inwards under the impact. She saw the self-repair seams spilt. She saw the blackness beyond, glimpsed through widening cracks and fissures.

She screamed.

Lana. Lana.

The voice grew loud, mingled with the tattoo of flailing fists against the hull. Again, the wall bent inwards. She stumbled back, hands over her ears but unable to block out his voice. Matt's voice. Pleading, begging and raging.

Lana. Lana. CommanderCommanderLanaLana Commandlana...

But this time Lana stood her ground

Stop it. Stop it. Fucking *stop it* –

The pounding grew louder and louder and then, suddenly, was silent and still. Lana stayed where she was. She heard her name, repeated over and again. She fought her breathing back under control. Someone was comming her.

Lana.

Go away.

Lana.

Shut up. Leave me alone –

"Lana."

"Chien?"

"We need to meet up." We? Oh yes, Chien and Isabella were definitely *we*. "We need to talk, all of us."

Lana glanced around. She was a long way from the command module. She was shaken. She needed to sit and drink coffee. Hot, strong coffee, ersatz, real, it didn't matter. "I'm close to the refectory." She strove to keep her voice steady. "I'll meet you and Isabella there. Kris? Kris? Can you hear me? Refectory, now."

*

The refectory was, of course, empty. It was an emptiness that drove in the reality of their situation like a nail into the skull. It was almost a taunt from the void. Look at you, the last. Pathetic and frightened. And alone, so absolutely alone. There should be off-duty crew in here, at ease, talking, playing of cards or chess, there should discreet romantic trysts in progress, but there was nothing, because the people who should have given this place life were all dead.

Chien and Isabella were already seated, their choice of table, arbitrary because none of the others were, or ever would be, occupied. There was no sign of Kris.

Lana headed for the coffee machine. "You two okay?"

Chien shrugged. "Yeah, I guess so."

"Coffee?"

"Already in hand." Isabella raised her cup to emphasise the point.

Kris arrived. They stood in the doorway, dishevelled, pale and nervous-looking then entered, drew out a chair and sat down. Lana joined them. She waited for what she considered to be a decent amount of time then said; "Chien, what have you found?"

"I've analysed the debris around the collision site," Chien said, "and found traces of explosives, and metallic compounds that are not part of the *Drake*."

Lana stared at the pilot, trying to make sense of the information. "Are you suggesting that the accident was no accident?"

"Yes."

"A collision with another vessel?"

"Unlikely, even back when the universe was crowded with stars and planets, spacecraft seldom hit each other. Space is just too big."

"You said that there were also traces of explosives? What does that mean? A projectile? A missile?"

"It's the only explanation I can come up with," Chien said. "I only found residue, scraps, but it was enough for me to identify it as human in origin."

"That makes no sense whatsoever," Kris said. Lana was glad to hear their voice. "There were no wars in progress when we left. No active terrorist groups, at least none capable of launching and guiding a rocket to a star ship. We would have been at quarter light speed by then, a fast-moving target."

Chien nodded and Lana could see the fear in the man's eyes. A reflection of her own, no doubt. "It would require the resources of a government to accomplish such a feat."

"Now I understand," Lana said.

"Understand?"

"Firstly, why I've been feeling that this is all wrong, too much of a coincidence."

"What are you talking about?" Chien said.

"If the collision killed the rest of the crew, why didn't it kill us? Think about it: Commander, pilot-navigator, engineer, and comms specialist and genetic engineer. What does that say to you?"

"The four disciplines needed to fly the ship and activate the protos," Kris said.

"Stroke of luck don't you think?"

"Not luck, murder," Chien said.

Lana didn't want to hear the word but if the collision had been deliberate then that was what it was.

"There's something else," Lana said. "When I prepared the stasis tanks for the funeral, I discovered that they hadn't failed because they were faulty or damaged by the collision, they failed because they were deactivated by the ship's AI."

"They were never intended to return from stasis." The first words Isabella had spoken.

"Exactly. They were killed by the *Drake*, or by whoever had programmed the AI to kill them."

"Why didn't you tell us this at the time?" Chien sounded angry.

"I...I wasn't certain. I needed more proof." A lie, but she had no other explanation to give them. And why was she trying to justify her decision to him anyway? She was the mission commander. Chien had no right to question her decisions. She was so bloody weak. She needed to get a grip.

"If all this is true then we were allowed to live only because we can fly the *Drake* to wherever it's meant to go." Isabella said.

"Okay, but if they need us, why target the hydroponics farm?" Kris said. "They've cut off our long-term food supply."

"That could simply be the impact point," Chien said. There was no warmth in his voice when he spoke to Kris. It was professional necessity, and nothing else. "We *were* a moving target. But I believe they targeted the farm deliberately."

"Why? If they need us alive, why starve us?"

"We're being herded, forced into something. Whoever did this knew we'd discover that the collision was no accident, so they need our co-operation. Starvation is a good motivator, don't you think?"

"And the temporal quantum jump?" Lana said.

"Deliberate. Iaen technology maybe?" Chien shrugged. "I need more coffee."

So do I, Lana answered silently. "I'll get it." She was glad to get to her feet, move away and carry out even this simple activity. She was also angry. If what Chien had found was true, then mass murder and coercion were taking place. The favoured tool of the fascist. Humankind's relationship with the Iaen, despite the technology they had gifted to their more primitive allies, had always troubled her. There was an inscrutability about the Iaen humanoid form that she had encountered more than once during her career. She suspected that something was being hidden from human eyes, although she had no idea what it might be.

She returned to the table and distributed the drinks. "So, Chien, what you're telling us is that the collision was an attack, that the crew were murdered and that the four of us are still alive for a reason."

"Yes. And you believe it too, don't you?"

"I don't want to, but yes, I do," Lana said. "What about you, Kris?"

"There are too many coincidences for it to be chance."

"There is a comfort in this," Isabella said.

"Comfort?" Kris said. "I can't see any possible –"

"Let her speak." An order, from Chien, and not a request. A reminder of the fragility of his relationship with Kris.

Lana tensed, waiting for Kris's reaction. Thankfully, they remained silent.

Isabella continued, "If we've been sent here on purpose, then it means that there must *be* a purpose, and that we're not meant to die."

"It depends on what that purpose is, but you're right, it might mean the difference between life and death for us," Lana said.

"Not for the rest of the crew it wasn't," Chien said. "They had no choice."

"But we do have choices. If we don't like what we are supposed to do, then we don't have to comply."

"We may *not* know," Chien said. "We've been manipulated since we launched."

"What we have to do is work together. All we have is a theory, a suspicion that we're being used. We have some evidence that the incident might have been deliberate, but even if it was, we don't know that the plan worked. This might not be where, or *when*, we're supposed to be. Our first duty, as a crew, and as living, breathing human beings, is to survive and I'm going to make damned sure that we do."

*

"Isabella," Kris had entered the command module. It was the day after the refectory conference. "Where's Chien? I need him to take a look at the navigation logs again." They had been avoiding the pilot, but could no longer do so.

"He went outside again." Isabella was at her station in the command module.

"I've been trying to comm him. I know he doesn't want to speak to me, but this is important. When did he go out?"

"Two…Oh God, two hours ago. He said he needed more samples from the collision point. I was listening. I didn't…" She had been lost in the dark again. Yearning for that voice. Chasing its whisper as it waxed and waned. "His life support will be running out. He'll die out there…"

"Hey, it's okay, Isabella. There's still time. I'll go and find him and bring him back. Comm Lana and tell her where I am and what's happening."

*

He needed to know that the void was empty. He needed to be sure that there was no threat out there in the night-black. As he stood guard on the upper hull of the *Drake*, staring deep into the heart of the darkness, Chien felt vindicated.

The monsters had already infiltrated the ship. He had seen them, crawling through the walls, swimming in the floor. It made him dizzy and nauseated to look at them. They made his head ache so intensely it felt as if his skull would crack. Then they would fade away, back out here to regroup, before another attack.

They were formed out of the dark itself, fearsome, hungry and energised by raw violence. They were the monstrous, like the truth they had uncovered. Too vast and terrible to comprehend.

It was an illusion. There was nothing out there and nothing in the Drake. *He should return to the airlock. This was foolish.*

And yet, if he didn't stand guard, who would? Who else was willing to protect the crew, to protect Bella? He had to face the night and whatever it hid.

You need to get back into the ship. Your air will run out soon.

He couldn't. Christ, he couldn't leave his post.

"Chien, what the hell are you doing out here?"

Kris's voice burst into the helmet comm. It was loud, startling and somehow crass.

"Go away. Leave me alone, Andersson."

"You must come back in, or you'll die."

Chien shook his head. No. No. Not yet. It wasn't safe.

He saw the bobbing glow of a helmet lamp. Presumably Kris trudging towards him over the curve of the hull. Determined. Aggressive. Angry. Yes, that was it. Angry because Chien had named them *he*, and called them out over the death of Nyung. Angry and insulted and looking to put things right. They were alone out here. Accidents happened.

Chien turned to face them.

His own name still hammered at him from inside the helmet. Confusing and uncomfortable. Oh, so you're pretending to care now are you, Andersson? Except you're blind to the truth of what we face, like all the rest of them. Even Bella. Even she won't listen.

Kris was suddenly close. They made a grab for Chien, who stepped back, as quickly as the suit would allow. Kris stumbled forwards, unbalanced by the clumsy movement. Chien swung about and slammed both hands into Kris's chest. The impact threw them both sideways. Chien fell. He rolled over the arc of the hull, towards the void. At any moment the ship's gravity would snatch him and hurl him down through the spokes to smash him into the hub. He grabbed wildly at the smooth metal, at nothing, at anything. There was only darkness and violent unstoppable motion.

Chien smacked into one of the transport tube supports. The thick fabric of the EVA suit absorbed the blow, but it left him stunned and disorientated.

*

The flashing life-support warning light on Chien's suit had been Kris's first sighting of him. The urgency of the signal drove Kris to unclip their lanyard and make a run for the navigator. They used the hull lamps and the soft glow of the transport tube as their guide. As Kris drew closer, their helmet light revealed that Chien was also unattached, teetering on the curved hull a few metres from the tube.

Kris almost collided with Chien but managed to skitter to a halt. They grabbed at Chien's arm, but the navigator stepped back out of reach. Then he swung around, and Kris felt an impact against their chest and fell.

*

Kris's voice once more hammered at him from the helmet commer. As Chien struggled back to his feet, out of breath and no longer able to draw in enough air to fill his labouring lungs, he realised that the engineer was calling for help.

He looked round wildly, scanning the hull with his helmet lamp but seeing nothing other than the endless curve of metal and the shadows cast by its landscape of external equipment.

No lanyard. The fool had come for him with no lanyard attached.

Me too. Think, you idiot. Think.

Chien fumbled the lanyard from its spool and attached it to the nearest protuberance.

His hands felt clumsy and stiff. The gloves did not allow for precision work, but this was something more than simple clumsiness.

Attached now, Chien set off over the shoulder of the hull. Kris still called for help over the commer. Their voice was a persistent irritation. They needed to shut up so that he could think. He needed to *think*.

There.

Kris, hanging from a sensor pylon, body flattened against the hull, feet dangling over nothing, arms taut as they fought the gravity field. Feeling as if his body weighed a thousand tonnes, Chien began an awkward descent towards the pylon.

*

The pain was unspeakable. It tore their shoulders and arms. It burned through them and screamed at them to let go. Kris looked down again and saw the darkness, a sea of nothing that clawed at them and pulled and pulled and pulled. Hands weakening, Kris waited for the end.

They heard voices. Chien, telling them to hold on, a little longer, just hold on. Chien, who had tried to kill them. Fucking Chien.

"Grab my hand."

What? They should take *his* hand?

Yes. Take it. Now.

Now.

Kris let go with their left hand and grabbed Chien's wrist.

Chien's oxygen level alarm bleeped into life.

Kris brought their own right-hand round and now hung from Chien's right arm. Now the pain belonged to Chien. He scrabbled at the lanyard spool with his free hand. It vibrated into life and they were in motion, dragged up over the curve and back to the antennae where the lanyard was anchored.

There they sat, crumpled and exhausted. Chien couldn't think straight. He was responsible for this but couldn't remember why or what had happened. He needed to take a deep breath, but he couldn't. He shallow-breathed, as if exhausted from a long, fast run. He was hot, clammy. Every joint in his body ached.

He needed to get out of this suit.

No, not yet. Not here.

Kris clambered to their feet then, without a word, turned about and headed towards the airlock. There was anger in the action.

Chien followed but found it hard to walk. He tried to call out to Kris over the commer but all that emerged was a croak. He couldn't remember how to talk. There were words but no mechanism to form them.

Oxygen. He needed oxygen.

The realisation broke into the confusion of thoughts and the incessant bleep of the life support failure

warning. Kris was too far away now. Chien staggered in
their wake, willing them to look back. They wouldn't.
They kept walking, over the curve of the hull,
disappearing onto the ladder to the airlock.

A million miles away.

He took what breath he could and shouted into the
commer. "She was my sister. Nyung was my sister and
you left her to die on Hoyle. You left her…You…"

*

Kris stopped dead and slowly turned around to stare at
Chien. His sister? Was that what this was all about? Was
that why he had tried to kill them?

They saw Chien drop to his knees, frantically
signalling. His hands went up to his helmet. The clasps.

Shouting into the commer, Kris ran towards him.
Someone else scrambled off the ladder and onto the hull
behind them. Kris glanced back to see Lana. Her lanyard
was attached. Good. They couldn't lose her. The thought
of it was unbearable.

Chien was on his back by the time they reached him.
He stared up at Kris, expression distraught behind the
visor. There wasn't much time. His air must be on the
verge of running out. Kris grabbed his arm. Lana caught
up and helped get Chien to his feet then she and Kris
supported him as they hurried back to the ladder.

*

"Fuck you, Chien. You tried to kill me."

In the airlock, now pressurised, its inner hatch open,
Chien slumped against the wall, helmet off and gasping
for air. Kris grabbed at the front of his suit and yanked
him up so that they could yell into his face, an explosion
of violence so sudden and unexpected it took both Lana
and Isabella several seconds to react.

"Kris, stop." Lana put her arm about their neck and
tried to pull the engineer away from Chien, but the EVA

suits they still wore made the attempt clumsy and almost farcical.

Isabella was shouting too and trying to shove herself between Kris and Chien. For a moment there was nothing but a struggle and raised voices. Then Lana managed to drag Kris back. They were still yelling, further out-of-control than Lana had ever seen them.

"You bastard."

"I…I had to make sure…I had to protect us…"

"What are you talking about, Chien?" Lana demanded.

Kris broke free of her and launched themself at Chien once more. Isabella took the brunt of the assault and pushed at Kris. She screamed at them, crying, and slapped their face. Kris stumbled to a halt, stood for a moment, shoulders hunched, fists clenched then stormed out of the airlock. Exhausted and shocked by her own outburst Lana ran in pursuit.

"Kris, Kris come back."

No response.

"Kris."

They stopped and swung round. "Fuck him, Lana. He tried to kill me. Fuck him."

"He's not well. We're all fragile. We're all…"

Kris shook their head then resumed their retreat. Ashamed of her weakness and anger, Lana returned to the airlock. Isabella knelt beside Chien who still gasped for air, eyes wide as if unsure where he was.

"What the hell were you doing out there?" Lana said.

Isabella was on her feet in a moment. "Leave him alone."

Lana recoiled. Isabella was near to tears, and furious. Lana bit down on her own anger at the other's disrespect. The last thing that was needed now was another fight.

"Sorry…I'm sorry," Chien said. He was breathless, his voice hoarse. "I…I had to be sure. I know it's not true. I know there's nothing out there, but I had to be sure."

"You're a fool Chi." Isabella held his face, crying now. "You could have died."

Lana decided to wait until Chien had recovered before

confronting him with his near manslaughter of Kris. The book said that she should take severe disciplinary action, but what use would that be out here? There were only four of them. They couldn't afford to lose any one of their number.

"Isabella, get Chien to his quarters. He needs to rest. Stay with him. We all need to stop and calm down."

*

Kris walked. They were exhausted, in need of sleep, but they couldn't stop. The moment they halted, leaned against the wall and closed their eyes they were back outside, hands clasped about the sensor tower, eternal nothingness beneath their feet as the weight of the gravity field dragged them down, always down. They should have let go. They should have fallen and embraced the peace of oblivion.

Eyes open.

Breathing hard.

Sweat-drenched.

There would be no rest. So, they walked.

Their father admired real men.

Why the hell were they thinking about their father? The bigoted old bastard was dead. He couldn't hurt them anymore. Now, that was a lie because he was here, in the lonely corridors of the *Drake*, in the emptiness inside as well as the infinite nothing outside. He stalked them and dripped all the old poison into Kris's ear. And yet, was just out of sight, just out of reach.

You should have died. You should have put an end to your misery. You should have let go and plummeted to your destruction. The coward taking the coward's way out.

You would have liked that, wouldn't you, you old bastard. The defective one put down, instead of your other son, the good one, Sven, the hero of the wars. Oh Sven, golden and perfect. The son who gave you the chance to bask in reflected glory, *reflected* because, my beloved father, you never did a glorious thing in your entire miserable, narrow little life. You drove a truck. You lived in the same town you were born in, one hundred and fifty-three miles from the Arctic circle.

Sven was a UN Marine, one of The Hellbringers who had recaptured Antarctica and broken the hold of the dissidents. He didn't come back.

The wrong one died.

You disgust me.

The words echoed through the empty corridor, loudly enough to stop Kris in his tracks.

You're weak Kris, You're pathetic. Pathetic and useless.

No. They were not going to listen to that bullshit anymore.

You're a man, so act like one.

A man.

My son. *A fucking* man. *You disgust me.*

I tried, on Hoyle, I tried, Dad.

But you left three of them behind didn't you. You shut the door in their faces and ran away...

Kris slumped back against the corridor wall then slid down until they sat on the floor, hunched double over their knees, arms over their head, wanting it to stop. Weeping until, exhausted by grief, they lay down on the hard, cold floor, foetus-curled, and drifted into sleep.

Which was where Lana found them an hour later.

*

"I want to beat him to a pulp. Christ, Lana, I was hanging on the edge of the pit."

They were together in Kris's bunk. In the dark. Entangled in each other's arms.

"And that'll help, will it? Fighting among ourselves?"

Kris didn't answer.

"He saved you, in the end," Lana said. "Why would he do that if he hates you so much?"

"I don't know. You're right. He could have left me to

die." Kris rolled onto their back, arm under their head. "I killed his sister."

"What?"

"She died because of me."

"Okay, Kris, you need to tell me what happened."

"No –"

"Yes. This time you do as I say, okay?"

"I can't."

"You can. And you will. Please Kris, I need to know."

Kris paused then began to speak. "I was engineer on the *de Gama*, after promotion and volunteering for everything. We were headed home from a cargo run to some godforsaken mining colony, when we received a distress call from a planet in the Canopus system –"

"Hoyle."

"Yeah, Hoyle. A massive eruption on the star's surface distorted its gravitational field and threw one of its planets out of orbit. It was on a collision course with Hoyle. There was a small scientific party on the surface, observing the star and the effect of the distortion on the planet. I stepped forward to take the lander down to evacuate them."

"That took guts, Kris."

"Like I said, I was ambitious and out to impress. It was a rough flight. Hoyle's own orbit had become erratic, and it was touch-and-go whether I'd hit its atmosphere at the right angle. And all the while that other lump of rock was bearing down on it.

"The surface was worse. Hoyle was beginning to break up. It was a young planet, a beautiful place. No civilisation but a couple of simian species that were using tools and showing signs of sentience. Now it was convulsed by catastrophic seismic activity, storms were ripping its atmosphere apart, but I managed to set the lander down in one piece on a grassy plain about a kilometre from the research party's last known position. We couldn't get closer because their observation site was on the flanks of a small mountain range, bordered by dense forest. They commed in that they were already making for the lander. I left the co-pilot behind and went out to meet them.

"That other planet filled a quarter of the sky, and it was coming in fast. There was a gale, dust, and smoke and ash from a huge volcano that had erupted about ten kilometres away. I found the research party, a few hundred metres into the forest. Trees were falling, torn branches lashing at our faces..."

...The lander. A dark shape in the storm. Hatch open, ramp down. Get the others in first. Kris Andersson, the rescue mission hero. See this, Dad? I'm a fucking hero.

Bleeding from uncountable nicks and cuts, therma parka ripped, hood up, back to the wind. Trying to remain on their feet as the ground trembled then heaved and bucked. Lightning whip-cracked into the ground. There was no shelter from it, just luck. The dust was like shrapnel, alive with rock chips and tree debris. The air was hot, thick and rotten with the stench of sulphur.

And all the time, that planet, a vast, cloud and dust-shrouded, horizon-wide dome, was swinging through space towards Hoyle like Lucifer's Hammer. It was dark and threaded with blazing red-hot wounds of its own. Gravitational forces would reduce both worlds to rubble long before collision.

Hurry up, come on, up the ramp, into the lander, leave your equipment. Go. Go. Go!

Kris's turn. Up the ramp.

Head count. Three short.

Another tremor. The lander seemed to slide sideways, its occupants thrown from their feet as they scramble for seats. Screams and cries of fear and pain.

Then a deep boom, like that of a titanic bell, that shudders through the lander. Something vast was happening somewhere on the planet, a massive injury, a fatal blow.

Time to launch and get away.

One of the scientists was shouting. "The others.

They're still out there."

"We have to go. Now."

"No, for God's sake, we have to wait a few more minutes. They're coming."

Kris palms the hatch pad. The ramp slides back up. Slowly, so, so, slowly. There are more booming sounds. The sky becomes a maelstrom of black, lightning-webbed cloud. There is fire, somewhere in the direction of the forest. A column of orange flame. Kris feels a wave of heat. The ground trembles.

The hatch slides across their line of sight.

And there, three figures, struggling through the chaos, barely discernible in the tornado of dust and debris, lit briefly by the maddened lightning and pursued by a tsunami of scalding orange-red lava that drowned the forest in liquid flame.

Too far away to save.

No time.

Hatch closed.

Passengers shouting, howling, in protest.

No time.

Launch. The lander bucks and shivers as it drives up into the storm.

Three left behind.

In Hell.

"You made the right call," Lana said, attempting reassurance but knowing it wouldn't work. Guilt that deep became the roots of your soul. She should know. "Those few moments could have cost all your lives."

"Don't you think I've tried to convince myself of that? It haunts my nightmares, Lana. It will never go away."

She tried to hold them, but Kris broke free and walked out. Lana didn't attempt to follow. They would come back when they were ready. Instead, she lay down and tried to find some sleep of her own.

*

The command module was empty. The corridors, vacant and silent but for the soft, life sounds of the ship, which hung motionless in the black. In the seed module, the protos floated in their womb fluids, unaware, un-alive and yet charged with the potential for life. Temperature and chemical balance monitored and adjusted.

The ship breathed. The ship functioned, dead, non-sentient but alive to changes and threat. It would continue to function until entropy ground its energies down to zero. Then it would go dark like the universe of which it was a miniscule component.

Another day. Two. Three. The crew, now coalesced into two pairs of lovers, withdrew from each other. They went about their business as best they could, but the fabric that held them together as a team had begun to unravel.

*

The empty command module was suddenly the loneliest place on the ship. Each station was deserted, but this was the place Isabella felt she was meant to be; at her post, where she listened.

The silence was no longer total. She could hear a new rhythm within her own body. Imagination perhaps, but she was sure there was a change to her heartbeat, to the spark and thrum of her nervous system. She smiled. She didn't care if it was simply wishful thinking, a delusion. It comforted her. If only she could sleep and not feel so nauseated.

Exhausted, she focused on the void.

And heard a whisper.

Isabella.

Her name. *He* knew her name. She felt tears prick her eyes. He had answered her at last. He was out there.

"Who are you?"

I am That I Am.

Now there was terror. *I am That I am*. The name God had given Himself when He spoke to Moses from the heart of the burning bush.

"Touch my soul," Isabella prayed silently. "Cleanse my unclean lips with hot coals as you did the lips of the prophet Isaiah."

You are forgiven, Isabella. You are my servant in whom I am well pleased.

Speak to me, God, please speak to me. Speak to my spirit.

Isabella...Isobel...Is...

The voice crumbled into a series of faint, irregular pulses, and washes of sound. YHWH, the sound of breath. The breath of life. God. Crying openly now, afraid that she was losing Him, Isabella focussed every part of her will on the sound. On the voice. On her God. It was difficult to hold. It waxed and waned. But it was there. She pleaded with Him to speak to her again and not leave her here, alone.

There. Again.

It *was* a song, and one she recognised.

"Commander. Lana, everyone. Command module. Now."

*

"A whisper?"

"Listen for yourself, commander."

Lana drew on the headset and closed her eyes. Her hands shook. At first, there was nothing but the peculiar roar of silence, then, deep in the nothing, a hiss, a faraway pulse.

"Is that a...?"

"Yes, a star," Isabella said.

"Can you be that sure?"

"A red giant. I know what I'm listening to."

"How far?"

"I would estimate it to be 30 lightyears, perhaps a little further."

"Why didn't you hear it before, Bella?" Chien asked. His voice was gentle. He seemed recovered, the professional once again, but with those sharp edges of his softened.

"I thought… I thought it was a voice."

"It is," Kris said. God, they looked ill.

"Is there enough signal for us to lock-on to its position?" Lana said.

"It will take a while," Chien took his place at the pilot's station. "Bella, send over what you've got."

"It's where we are supposed to go," Kris said.

"We don't know that for sure."

"Come on, Lana. We happen to be a few lightyears from a star in a dark universe. Stroke of luck, don't you think?"

"I don't care what it is. I'll reserve judgement until we get there."

"It's a risk," Kris said. "A quantum jump might take us even further forward in time. There's another factor here. Those signals are 30 years old. It could be an echo from a dead star."

"It's a star," Lana said. "It's a destination. We have nowhere else to go."

"Unlikely to have habitable planets," Chien again.

"Unlikely is not impossible." Lana said. "As for the quantum drive, we don't use it. We use the ions instead and go into stasis." That would mean a journey of around 50 years, but what had they got to lose?

When they returned there would be a star shining down on the *Drake*. There would be light. There would be *something*.

"With all due respect, commander," Kris, of course. "We have to weigh up the risks involved in taking that journey, against staying here and working to get home. Ion flight puts a strain on the ship's super-structure and systems. There's been a lot of damage, we don't know if the *Drake* will survive the voyage." He glanced around at Isabella and Chien, as if looking for their support. "When, and if, we get to that star and it's still viable, what then? The chances of there being an inhabitable planet in orbit around a red giant are slim. Its inner planets, anything in its Goldilocks Zone, would have been swallowed up when it collapsed and expanded into its present state. Any survivors would be its outer planets; rock and ice worlds, or gas giants."

"All taken into account." Lana kept her voice steady, and took a moment before continuing. "But, realistically, Kris, Chien, how close are you to finding us a way back?"

Chien spoke up. "We're up against a dead end. It looks as if the engineering and navigation logs, everything, in fact, were wiped at the moment of collision and there is nothing until a few weeks before we returned. Whoever did this to us didn't want us to know how to get home."

"Isabella?" Lana said. "What are your thoughts on what we should do? It's your star."

"We'll name it after you," Chien said.

"Romance at the end of the universe," Lana was glad to notice the mood lighten slightly. Even Kris managed a brief, tight smile.

"I think we should go," Isabella said. "We are going to run out of food, despite your makeshift garden, Lana, because it will be a long time before we can grow enough for us to eat. There might be a habitable planet. It might provide a source of food. The ship might break up during the journey, but if we're in stasis we won't be aware of that. The odds are against us, but it's a risk worth taking. I'd rather die trying than starve to death out here." Isabella paused before she continued. "There's something else none of you have considered. Our cargo. Our mission. We must assume that humankind has long since died out. I have picked up no radio signals or other communication, current or echo, to indicate our species ever existed, let alone still survives. We're close enough to home, spatially, to pick up some whisper, from starships, colonies, Earth itself, but there is nothing. I have sent out distress calls. No reply. Silence. We are alone."

Lana closed her mind to the hellishly vast implications of that truth.

"We don't have to be the last," Isabella continued. "We have the means to survive on an airless planet –"

She was right. The landers would serve as accommodation, along with a set of pre-fabricated domes, carried by the *Drake* and intended as a colony beachhead encampment.

"– and we can then modify the protos for the planet's environment," Isabella said. "They will have access to our logs and knowledge banks, and the landers. So, it wouldn't be long before they become a space faring species."

"To what end?" Kris said. "The universe is dead, Isabella."

"Dark," Isabella said. "Not dead."

"There's a difference?"

"Yes. What is the point of anything? Even in a universe filled with light and teeming with living things? There is no God. I couldn't find Him. I listened. I begged Him to speak." She sounded close to tears now, tears and breaking point. "The only purpose for anything is life and we have the means to grant humankind a rebirth."

Chien had crossed to her and slid his arm about her shoulders. Isabella smiled up at him then continued. "There is another reason for us to survive." She paused as if gathering her courage. "I'm pregnant."

*

Later, as the lid of her stasis tank slid shut, Lana had just enough time to comprehend that this may be her last moment of consciousness before her death.

PART TWO

And there was light.

On the vid screen, complete and alive, its glare filtered to a hellish blood-red. Solar flares rose and arced over the curve of the star's circumference, stark against the blackness in which it hung. The surface seethed and boiled as it consumed the last of its diminishing fuel through its millennia-long death rattle.

No one spoke. The crew, freshly returned, simply sat at their stations and stared at the screen. They drank in what they saw. A dying star, bloated, cool and vast. A red ember, defiantly swollen, teetering on the edge of collapse.

A star.

Light.

Lana blessed the *Drake*. It had brought them here, safely, but at great cost. Kris's first-awake report had not been encouraging. Their voice had been edged with an emotion that sounded like grief.

"The *Drake* is failing faster than I had thought it would. The deterioration is speeding up. The ship is tired. It's held itself together by sheer willpower, if such a thing is possible, but this last voyage broke it."

Many of the wounds in the hull had re-opened. Several modules were without life-support and therefore unusable. The vessel's systems were collapsing one by one.

Transfixed as they were, by the star, no one had listened fully, or comprehended the seriousness of their situation. Tears ran down Isabella's cheeks. Chien's arm was about her shoulders as they stood before the screen and gazed at the light. His eyes were bright with something that resembled joy. Kris stood next to Lana. She felt their hand close about hers.

Light.

The darkness broken. Energy, heat. It was too vast to fold into words or feelings.

Then, just as the wonder began to dim and the parlous state of their starship registered on the crew's consciousness, Isabella, back at her station, reignited their euphoria with more good news.

"I've found planets."

It was almost too much to bear. Not only a lonely, solitary star, but planets. This time however, the flare of hope died quickly, because the chances of any of them being capable of sustaining life was slim. In their fragile condition, the crew's morale was in danger of a collapse as acute as their ascent into euphoria.

"Listen up," Lana overrode her own bleakness. "We've made it here. The *Drake* is in a bad way but capable of keeping us alive for a while longer. There are planets. Chien and Isabella will find one for us, ideally one we can settle on, but if all else fails, one we can, at least, land on. Kris, your responsibility is to keep the *Drake* in one piece for a while longer."

"I'll do my best," they said.

"Everyone, remember Jupiter's moon, Io is…was…predicted to become a new earth-type world when our own sun went red. Betelgeuse 15, Ling Shao's Planet, both of them viable worlds in a red giant solar system."

"There's another factor to consider," Kris said. "If what we suspect is true, there's something waiting for us here. We need to decide if we meekly go along with our puppet masters or leave well alone."

"You mean, we die up here." Chien, his voice ice-cold.

"If necessary, yes."

"I don't believe I am hearing this. You want us to give up and die?"

"Hear him out," Lana said. She didn't want to. She wanted them to find a planet they could call home and bask in its crimson daylight. But a devil's advocate was needed here, to bring some perspective and realism to their dangerous joy.

"Thank you, Lana. Look, whoever's behind this has shown themselves to be utterly ruthless. Which means that we could be here to carry out some terrible act."

"What kind of terrible act would that be, Andersson?" Chien said. "There nothing here. The universe is dark and cold and empty. Who the hell can we hurt except each other?"

"Kris is right," Lana said. "But do we have a choice?"

"No, we don't," Chien said.

"So, you think we simply do as we're told. Is that it?" Kris was on their feet, tone and posture aggressive.

Exasperated at the provocation, Lana pulled rank. "That's enough, Kris." She then addressed the entire crew. "We go in with our eyes open and try to second guess what the puppet masters have planned."

"Or," Kris said, "we go into stasis and let the *Drake* die."

"No," Isabella said. "We don't give up. We are life. We carry life. Surely our responsibility is to perpetuate it at all costs."

Lana was suddenly exhausted. Time to bring the debate to a conclusion. "We have to make up our minds fast, or the *Drake* will decide for us."

*

Later, her watch over, Lana retired to her cabin. There were no shadows, no ghosts. The presence of light outside, the breaking open of the unutterable darkness, seemed to have wiped away her imaginings. The hallucinations were like a fever dream now.

She lay down, closed her eyes, and let the tears come. Lana felt guilt. She had nothing to offer the crew other than the vain hope of finding a planet that was even minimally habitable, the deadly journey surface-wards if one was discovered, or a peaceful death in the stasis tank. Whatever the outcome, she had brought them to their final destination.

But there was an unspoken hope. There was a tacit agreement that this was where they were meant to be. There was something waiting for them in this lonely solar system.

But how did the planners know?

Alone in her ready room, Lana pushed the question aside and allowed herself to weep for Matt. One moment he had been breathing, thinking and *being*, the next shattered into a million fragments, hurled apart by the force of the explosion. His remains mingled with atomised metal, burning fuel and the microscopic shards of his crewmates. Part of him fell, like bloody rain, through the dense, toxic atmosphere of Venus. Part of him was blasted outwards across space and, unless snatched by the gravity of some planet or sun, still travelled the void.

She wept for Matt, yes, but also for her world. The people, the civilisations that had evolved so painfully and bloodily over Earth's long, yet brief, history. Its heights, its triumphs all gone now, humankind's relentless drive forwards and onwards, all for nought, because everything was dead and frozen in the darkness.

And not just humankind, but the countless other civilisations scattered across the universe. Even the godlike Iaens, who had given humankind so much, were dust now, remembered by no one, except four humans on a doomed starship.

But here was a sun. Here were planets. Perhaps life could cling to this last outpost of light and warmth, a last-minute reprieve for humankind. And if a sun survived here, then there might be others far off in the suffocating blackness.

Was that hope? Or desperation?

Lana was commed sometime late into her sleep period. It was Isabella.

"We've found it, and it has oxygen and water."

*

"There are seven planets. This one has an approximate circumference of 43,000 kilometres, so it is a little larger than Earth. It is 60 AUs from the sun, well into the red giant's Goldilocks zone."

The crew were once again gathered in the command module. Lana could tell that Isabella was excited but trying to temper it with realism.

"The planet is tidally locked."

Orbit and rotation synchronised to create a permanent bright side and dark side. Disappointing.

"The other planets?"

"Two are too close to the star and one is too far away. The remaining two are gas giants," Isabella said. "Including one that's twice the size of Jupiter."

"All right." Lana took her seat and activated her station. "Take us there, Chien, and let's have a closer look."

*

It was a speck at first. Imagined before it blinked into wispy, distant life on the screen. It grew steadily into a tiny disc that glittered against the formless, solid black.

Kris was silent, pale and tense at their engineering station, as if they were trying to hold the ship together with their bare hands.

Features began to appear; clouds, dark and ochre swirls of rock and desert. No greens. No blues. White crusts over the poles, more white patches here and there over the surface. Ice? Water? Always the hope of water.

Atmosphere analysis, low levels of oxygen, like the upper reaches of a mountain on Earth. Thin, which would make it hard to function and produce adverse physiological effects, but survivable for short periods. Oxygen masks required, but no need for full EVA suits.

Brightside temperature 200°C at the equator, so not survivable, but that was rendered academic when radiation readings came in. Levels were lethal. The dark side, still high but survivable in moderate doses. A subterranean existence would be advisable.

Dark side it was then.

More darkness.

No sun.

No stars. Perhaps a glimpse of those neighbouring planets.

But no stars.

And a brutal truth.

It was Isabella who voiced it. "One of us has to stay on

the *Drake* to prepare and protect the seed module until the landing party has enough data for me to engineer the protos."

They were in the Drake's hangar module, loading-up the landers ready for planetfall.

A moment, then Kris said; "It should be me. I'm the engineer. I know this ship –"

"No," Isabella said. "I have to do it."

There was a moment, a fraction of a second in which Lana simply accepted the fact. Then she remembered where they were, when they were and who they were. This was of immense significance. If Isabella could carry the child to term, then the four of them would not be the last naturally born humans in the universe. There was something almost Biblical in the concept.

"It's early. This my first child," Isabella continued. "The chances of a miscarriage are high. Planetfall is rough, so I don't want to go through it twice. And, with all due respect to you Kris, we all have engineering training. You're the specialist, yes, but I can keep the *Drake* together for long enough. And, if something happens and I'm the only one left, I can still use whatever data I do have to partially engineer the protos and then fly the seed module down to the surface." A hard truth but a logical one. Isabella had thought this through.

She was also right. "I don't like leaving you here alone," Lana said.

"She won't be alone," Chien moved in to take Isabella's hand. "I'm staying with you, Bella."

"We need you on the surface, Chien. And you're the best pilot we have."

"Andersson is a good pilot." A simple statement but it felt like a breakthrough. Lana knew, however, that it was far from a precursor to a tearful reunion between the pilot and the engineer. "I'm not leaving Bella, or my child." There was a finality in Chien's voice. Lana knew she was defeated. She could order him to come with her and Kris. She could demand and shout, but it would encumber them with a distracted pilot and colleague. Chien was fragile, they all were. Tearing him away from the woman he obviously loved could break him.

Lana sighed. "Okay, okay. Perhaps you're right. And two pairs of hands are better than one up here. Kris, you take Lander Alpha, I'll take Beta. Remember, there are immense ramifications to this. You could say that Isabella is the new Eve, not that she wants that responsibility on her shoulders. But it does mean that the argument over whatever black ops mission this might be, is moot now. We have a new life to prepare for and nurture. *That* is our mission."

*

Planetfall in a lander was always terrifying, no matter how many descents a pilot had made. The launch from the catapult rails in the hangar was exhilarating. Igniting the drives, even more so; that push into the back, the increased gees, all part of the thrill. A hard flat turn, more gees, then Lana glimpsed the *Drake*. Debris tumbled about her like miniature moons. There was the flicker of flame visible through re-opened wounds in her hull. The quantum drive ring was turning dull as it failed. A moment of grief, then, for the ship, their home, womb and protector that had done all it could to keep its human inhabitants safe. A moment later the planet filled the front port and rushed in at alarming, but still exhilarating speed.

Auto-pilot systems brought the lander up to the correct angle. Little margin of error, too steep and there was a fiery death. Too shallow and the lander would bounce and skitter off into space. The latter was a survivable mistake. The former offered no second chances.

Then it was down into the atmosphere. The terror started early on, as the lander's belly was warmed by friction. The craft began to shudder and buck then suddenly it was a superheated, trembling, bouncing monster, barely under the pilot's control and dead to all outside communication.

A meteorite.

A fireball.

Lana held on. She had long lost sight of Kris's lander and could see little but the halo of yellow-white heat that curled about her own lander's nose. Her gaze flickered over the instrumentation. Speed. Angle. Altitude. Temperature. Structural status. The craft rocked and staggered, overloaded, heavy and cumbersome.

The flames grew higher, whiter. The madness increased until she wanted to scream.

This is when Matt died. At the peak of re-entry. At the worst moment. When his lander was under maximum structural and heat strain.

It ended.

The shudder and roar slid away and the lander soared above the planet's rough, rocky landscape. It raced through its red-tinged twilight, over razor ridged outcrops and towering stone spires that cast long, deep shadow onto each other's flanks and across the flat plains of folded, long-frozen lava fields.

The twilight darkened until it was night. Everlasting night. The lander's beams flicked on. Lana saw Alpha, ahead and to her left. The navigation lights described the lander's outline. Lana's radar showed it as a green triangle, sliding slowly across the screen.

Her own navigation systems locked on tightly to Kris's lander and followed it through the dark.

Lana hated the darkness.

Lana hated all darkness.

A lurch, a shudder. She felt the lander dip to the right. Alarms brayed. Warning messages flashed on the panel. *Starboard drive malfunction. Starboard drive shutdown. Shutdown. Shutdown. Shutdown.*

"Lana? Are you okay?" Kris's voice, breaking into the cacophony.

"I've lost a drive."

"Switch to glide mode. We can set-down in seven minutes. Glide mode."

Lana was flight-simulator-trained. Emergency

procedures had been drummed into her. Yet she couldn't think, not here in the pitch black. Her hands were frozen.

Come on. *Move.*

Glide mode.

She flicked her eyes across the sight-panel and blinked; here, here and here.

Another warning. She shut down the other engines. Flaps trimmed. Nose up. Catch whatever atmosphere was out there. Let it bear the lander up. Six more minutes. Five. Four...

Too fast.

The lander was overloaded. Its extra mass gave the craft unwanted momentum.

Twenty seconds. Firing VTOL thrusters. Forward momentum still too high. The thrusters unbalanced the lander. Its nose dropped, its tail end arced skywards and threw Lana forward in the straps. She glimpsed more of those lava folds in the glare of the nav lamps then braced as alarms shrieked.

The lander slammed into the ground and felt, for a moment as if it rested, not-quite vertical, on its nose cone. It wavered there for a long half-second, teetered between completing its summersault over onto its back and crashing back onto its belly. Then, the moment ended, the cone disintegrated and, VTOL thrusters still firing, the lander reared upwards, nose first then dropped backwards. The jets slowed its descent, but not enough to prevent it slamming its belly onto the ground and with enough force to shock Lana into a darkness of her own.

*

When she saw light again, it brought confusion, and pain. There were voices. There were hands on her. She panicked. Where were they taking her? What were they doing to her? She lashed out, feebly. What she thought was bright, light daylight was the crazed bobbing of an EVA helmet lamp. The voices were muffled. A babble. Then the pain won. It felt as if her skull was being prized apart. It felt as if her entire body had been broken. She wanted to be sick. She wanted to lie down. She wanted to be left alone. But the light and voices and rough hands wouldn't go away. They dragged at her and there was fresh pain. Hot flashes that lanced through her.

Unbelievably, cruelly, she was hauled up onto her feet. She couldn't stand. Someone held her up. She rested on them. They dragged her. She tried to walk but her legs were tangled. They didn't belong to her. They felt too far away from her to control. Someone shut her helmet visor again. She was afraid. She was trapped in here, in the suit. Yes, suit. EVA suit.

Her head began to clear. Now there was a loud ringing sound in her ears. The sound hurt. Every movement and every breath hurt. She saw wreckage, wires, boxes, strewn about her. The hatch was only half open. She was breathing too fast and hard.

Outside the lander. Yes, that was where she had been, in the lander.

The lander.

The crash.

Which meant that she was alive.

Jesus. She was alive!

Outside. Dark. Always dark. She loathed the blackness. But there were, after a few moments, shapes out here. A slight glow. A slight lessening of the black. And ahead, the bulk of the other lander.

It was Kris who dragged and supported her across the rough ground.

She felt a little stronger. She could move her legs now. She could walk but still needed to lean on Kris.

Did it matter.

It did.

It didn't.

Then they were on the ramp limping up towards the surviving lander's hatch.

And a bunk.

God, she needed to lie down.

And suddenly she did. She didn't remember getting

here. Her helmet was off, her suit. Someone leaned over her.

"Commander? Lana?"

Kris. It was Kris. Lana mumbled something to them. Kris smiled. They smiled and Lana loved that smile. Then Kris kissed her forehead. And all was well.

*

Isabella and Chien were up in the hangar's tiny flight control cabin from where they had watched the landers' launch, and now waited for the great doors to slide back into place. They wouldn't be able to venture back into the area until the air pressure in the hangar itself was restored to safe levels.

They were alone.

And yet not.

There was life inside Isabella. Primitive, unformed and as yet unliving, just a few cells, dividing, as its DNA sculpted it into something vaguely human.

"We should get to the seed module," Chien said. His hand was tight about hers.

Isabella nodded her agreement but felt too tired to move. Instead, she sat down at the cabin's command station, alert to alarms, watching the readings that slid across the screens. More areas were being shut down. Great lengths of the curved hull had ruptured. The seed module was still intact and unscathed, however. That was all that mattered.

Chien crouched beside her. "All right, we'll go when you're ready," he said, with the gentleness of a tamed wild animal. That was what she had done to him, calmed him, given him something to live for.

She closed her eyes. Voices, music and the whispers filtered into her awareness. When she opened them again, she glimpsed flickering movements in the floor and curved walls of the module.

Then, before she could comprehend what was happening, the first of the cramps hit her.

She cried out. Unable to move. Eyes open. Confused.

The baby.

Oh God, no, please.

"Chien, something's wrong."

The first cramps had been dull punches to her abdomen.

Chien grabbed her hand. He seemed unable to speak. She didn't care. His presence was enough.

She waited for the cramp to pass. They weren't physically agonising, but the implications were. She felt a sudden damp warmth between her thighs. It burned.

Blood.

She wanted to cry but fought against the urge.

"I think I'm losing it…losing the baby…"

*

There were things in the walls.

In the *walls*.

They were shadows that slithered and boiled in a never-ending shapeshifting dance. They twisted and writhed in a strange grey world revealed through translucent windows that had once been plain metal bulkheads and inner hull.

Isabella wondered why she felt no fear.

I can heal you.

Heal me? Heal the child? Give it back to me?

I can heal you.

First person, singular and yet she could feel the presence of many.

Many and yet one.

As God was three yet one.

Yes, she said, silently because she was sure that the spoken word was unnecessary. They/it knew. They/it could hear her.

"Bella, are you okay?" Chien sounded frightened.

And he was. The walls were again alive with movement, with the silhouettes of unthinkable beings, with threat and terror. With monsters, at last emerging

76

from the darkness. They were everywhere, in the cabin, in the hangar. They hurt. They drove into Chien's skull and poured in liquid pain. His stomach clenched. He was dizzy. He couldn't think for all the cacophony in his head; voices, laughter, gunfire, screams.

Then a figure unfolded itself from the madness that swirled and danced through the floor. It reared to its full height, three-metres or so, and towered over Chien. The creature was vaguely human, hairless, with blank dark eyes, a rough-hewn, oversized imitation that looked as if someone had made a half-hearted attempt to mould clay into a statue. The thing seemed to fill the cramped little space. The patterns and shapes in the room's walls and floor flowed through its skin and formed a connection between the figure and the maelstrom from which it was created.

Chien recognised it.

Iaen.

*

Isabella got to her feet, shakily, uncertain and still holding herself tightly with her arms, as if, somehow, that would stop the tragedy her body was enacting. She stood, not knowing what she was supposed to do. Pray? Plead?

To me. Come to me.

There was an Iaen in the room.

Chien stood between it and Isabella, as if trying to prevent it from getting to her. Tough as he was, he stood no chance against the Iaen. There was threat here, but Isabella didn't understand what it was. Surely, the Iaens were humankind's friends. This one was surely here to help, although only God knew how it had found its way onto the ship.

"I want to heal you," it said. Its voice was deep and caused a ripple to shimmer through the maddening shapes that inhabited the fabric of the room.

"How? It's too late."

"No."

She knew then, somehow, and sank to her knees. She felt a pulsing warmth in the floor. The Iaen stepped past Chien, who had no choice but to move aside. It reached down and gently, but firmly, pushed Isabella forwards until she was prone, the length of her body pressed against the serpentine shadows, which were now angels with vast, outspread wings.

"No. Leave her alone." Chien threw himself at the Iaen who swept its arm round to slam him into the control station. Stunned and bruised Chien struggled to his hands and knees and watched, helpless to save the woman he loved.

Isabella felt the things reach into her. She felt pain as parts of her knitted and reformed. She sobbed but refused to cry out. Her body was ablaze with lancing bolts of electric shocks. She *felt* the restless shadows and, for a moment, was part of them. She gasped as the pain reached a climactic white heat. It stiffened her body, clenched her teeth and drew a sob of agony from deep within.

She glimpsed Chien struggle to his feet and move towards her and the Iaen. She shook her head. She didn't want it to hurt him again.

Then it was over.

She lay, still and exhausted, but was at peace, content and not alarmed as the Iaen humanoid crumbled and dissolved to dust. Its demise seemed inevitable and as things should be.

Beneath Isabella's weariness lay an odd meld of euphoria and unease. She knew that the foetus had been restored. She felt it. Heard it, was gripped by an utter, joyous certainty that was impossible to explain. Her unease arose from what she had seen and discovered. They had attempted to hide the truth from her, deep, deep within themselves, but she had not been afraid to fall into their darkness as she had fallen into the darkness outside the ship. She now knew how to listen and now she knew what the Iaens wanted and why they were here, in the final darkness, orbiting this last and lonely planet.

"Isabella, look."

Chien's voice held something that was almost grief. Isabella lifted her head and saw the living Iaen tapestry turn dark grey, then black as if polluted by great ink spots that seeped outwards to snuff out the never-still dance of shapes. Isabella felt them die. There was no pain or horror, but acceptance. They were part of the ship and the ship was part of them and now the *Drake* was plummeting towards its demise, so were the beings that gave it life.

They had served their purpose. They had brought humankind to the end of the universe.

Isabella knew why, but the knowledge was a confusion of images and voices. It was like a dream, vivid while inhabited by the sleeper but dissolved into meaningless fragments once the sleeper woke.

*

They had made planetfall a hundred metres or so from a vast expanse of ice. A quick analysis revealed the ice to be fresh water that could be purified and made drinkable. The rocky shore of this frozen lake was approximately half a kilometre wide and bordered by a cliff wall about thirty metres in height. The cliffs were overshadowed by mountains, dark, formless and oppressive, even in the glare of the lander lamps. An initial expedition to the cliffs revealed rockfalls and immense cracks, one of which had left a grand natural arch about a kilometre to the south. The arch gave entrance into the mountain range.

All this was revealed by the light of hand, head and body lamps attached to the arctic parkas Lana and Kris wore over their therma-tunics. There was no natural light. The darkness closed in the moment any lamp beam was moved on to a different subject. The sky was black and blank. No stars. No planets visible. No moon.

The dark was not total, however, but alleviated by a faint red glow on the horizon, far beyond the furthest reach of the ice lake. It was a glimpse of the planet's massive sun. The star cast no illumination on the landing site but offered comfort. It was a reassurance that there was still light in the universe, even if it was the final gasp of a dying stellar ember.

The planet was cold enough to freeze human lungs if a combined thermal and oxygen face mask wasn't worn. A therma parka and tunic were vital for any time spent outside. The atmosphere was breathable but thin, which meant that the crew were able to spend short periods outdoors without a life support tank, if necessary, but a lightweight pack was advisable and made life a lot easier.

Radiation levels here on the nightside were higher than ideal, but the therma-tunics were designed to protect them from the worst of it. It posed no immediate threat, but it was unlikely that any of them would live beyond their sixties. The heat and radiation on the day side, however, would be instantly lethal.

Kris drilled core samples from the beach then analysed them in the hope that perhaps they might contain nutrients necessary to plant growth. Their initial findings were hopeful. The igneous rock could, if powdered and mixed in with the crew's own waste, be used as soil. Lana set to work on the makeshift troughs she had manufactured on the ship. She filled them with a mix of soil, faeces and crushed rock then planted seeds. They were watered with melted ice from the lake. The lamps in the surviving lander would have to suffice as a light source.

In the meantime, she and Kris ate processed powders and pastes from the *Drake's* food store.

The next task was the construction of the interlinked complex of three prefabricated dome dwellings that formed the bridgehead camp. The components had been carried in Lana's lander and were, thank all the known gods, undamaged by the crash. The landers were built for rough travel and hard landings. It was also the reason Lana, though still bruised, stiff, and prone to headaches and lander-crash flashbacks, was still alive. The external shell absorbed the shock, and the inner shell protected the lander's contents. The crash seat cushioned the body from the extremes of planetfall.

Radiative sky cooling provided the electricity for their campsite.

Once the camp was set-up and the plant troughs transferred to one of the domes, Kris set about itemising parts from the crashed lander for cannibalisation. The derelict would also be used as extra accommodation during their stay here.

Stay.

A friendly, lightweight word. Suggestive of vacation, or brief visit. A word preferred to sojourn, lifetime, exile. A self-deluding word that each of them used to describe their presence here. Neither of them even considered naming the planet.

*

"We need to take a look round." Lana said.

It was the first evening. Exhausted from their day's labour, Lana and Kris were in the dome they had chosen as their domicile. Evening was, of course, meaningless in terms of planetary rotation. Time periods here were measured in synch with *Drake* time.

"I'm worried about Isabella and Chien," Kris said. "We should take the readings we need and get back to the ship as soon as possible."

"We need to find a cave to give us greater shelter from the radiation. And there's oxygen and water, which means that there might be life here. We need to look for evidence."

"Life, maybe, but somehow, I don't think there's much going on here in the way of sentience."

"That's a big assumption to make," Lana said.

Although, she admitted silently, Kris was probably right. This really was a desolate lump of rock, half of it frozen, the other baked and radioactive. Life here wasn't going to be easy even with all their equipment and technology. Yet, Lana's morale was higher than it had been for a long time. This moment with Kris had an air of honeymoon about it. Alone, here in the dome, working together they were warm and comfortable with each other. And yet, Lana recognised that the good feeling was shallow, a veneer laid over the horror of the empty universe and their utter aloneness. There was a sense that this world was home now, but at the same time, a fragile beachhead. She wondered how Isabella and Chien were coping up there in the *Drake*. She missed them and wanted them here, safe on the surface.

"Tomorrow, then," she said.

There was, she knew, a third reason for the expedition. The need to keep moving forward, pushing outwards.

Wasn't that the human condition?

And there were, after all, still humans in the universe.

*

They entered the foothills through the natural archway, which, for Lana at least, marked a transition between the small relatively safe world they had already made for themselves on the beach and a vast, lightless unknown.

A rough trail led away from the arch and wound between the steeply sloped rock faces. Glimpsed in the lamp beams the mountains resembled titanic statues. Boulders were piled at the bases of the rock walls. Presumably the detritus of landslides.

Lana walked ahead of Kris. Determined not to falter. She felt clumsy in the big parka and could hear little more than her own breath and the occasional comm from Kris. It was easier to communicate that way, it was difficult to talk through the mask.

They were armed. Lana had assented to Kris's request reluctantly but saw the logic of it. If there was life here, it might not be the kind you could reason with. However, she had made it clear that they were not to draw a firearm, let alone fire it, unless their backs really were to the wall. Even then, warning shots only.

The trail was surprisingly level and smooth. No fissures or loose gravel. There were the occasional patches of white, frozen water.

"Lana, to your left." Kris broke several minutes of comm silence. "Looks like a cave."

Lana swung her lamp round and there, a few metres above a landfall of rocks, was a large opening in the rock face.

"Okay, let's take a look."

Lana took a breath then clambered onto the landfall and climbed towards the cave entrance. Every part of her body ached. The battering she had received from the crash was taking its toll. Her head ached. She felt nauseated but fought it down. She couldn't falter. Her crew needed her. She battled her way over the last rough stairway of boulders and up to the cave entrance. Kris arrived a few seconds ahead of her. They waited. She noticed that their hand was on the handle of their weapon. Lana shook her head.

They lifted their hand away.

A moment, while Lana recovered her breath, a nod then they stepped inside. The darkness here was complete. As crushing as the outer darkness of space had been during her spacewalk, a few days...no, half a century ago.

The lamps revealed a high arched roof from which stalactites reached downwards, their slow growth forever stalled because the water needed to feed them was frozen. There were thousands of them, fang-like and ghost white. Stalagmites formed intricate, miniature mountain ranges on the floor, and made Lana feel as if she was in the jaws of some titanic carnivore.

There were smaller cave mouths at the rear, entrances to tunnels that led deeper into the mountain.

And something else.

Great pale and fleshy semi-circles clung tenaciously to the cave walls. The largest of them were almost two metres in lateral diameter and projected almost a metre from the rock face. Lana moved towards it to confirm her first impression. "Fungi," she said. "How the hell can it grow here?"

"Nutrients in the rock," Kris said. "Fungi can grow anywhere. It was even found in the Chernobyl nuclear power station after the disaster in the twentieth century The point is –"

"Can we eat it?" Lana said.

She heard Kris's soft chuckle. That was unexpected. They didn't laugh often. "Exactly." They reached up and sliced off a small segment with a knife produced from inside their parka. It was a vicious-looking tool, large enough to double as a weapon. Kris dropped the sample into a bag and placed it in their belt pack.

"Are you up for going deeper?" Lana said.

"Absolutely."

The tunnel was circular, about two and a half metres from curved floor to arched ceiling and surprisingly even and straight. There were sections where they had to crouch and, in one place, almost bend double. Lana was once again in front. The place made her uneasy. They were trapped down here.

By what?

There was more fungus, and what looked like fine roots growing on the surface of the rock. The fungus filament system perhaps? The air down here was damp. The walls glistened with ice. Lana made sure they moved slowly and carefully. An injury down here would be catastrophic. She wanted to turn back but she was driven on by some inner demon that urged her to go just a little further. Then a little further. There was something at the end of this and she needed to know what it was.

And whether it was friend or threat.

She caught sight of another entrance, or exit, ahead of them, a circle of black that the lamp wouldn't penetrate from this distance. That meant that either there was a sharp bend in the cave or that it opened out into a chamber of some description. She slowed as they drew near then raised her hand as a signal for Kris to stay where they were. She moved cautiously. Another pause. Another breath. She sensed that there was a large space on the other side of the circle.

Lana stepped through onto a ledge that overlooked a large, high-roofed chamber. Stalactites hung in great swathes like white organ pipes in a giant cathedral. As she played the lamp over its interior, she saw movement.

Something scuttled out of the light. Startled and unnerved she tried to follow it with the lamp, not *wanting* to see what it was, but knowing that she *had* to.

There, again, seemingly frozen in the light.

Her first impression was of an arachnid. A large ovoid body. Multiple, long, chitinous legs.

Another.

This one froze as if pinned in place by the glare of her lamp.

Arachnid, yes, but with a torso and head that gave it a centaur-like appearance. That head, however, was little more than a vehicle for its jaws. The creature was some two metres in length although the leg span was a lot more. There were no eyes and yet Lana could feel its regard. It knew she was there. It was focussed on her. Transfixed. Perhaps the light was painful to it.

Painful or not, there was no way Lana was going to move the lamp away. She needed to know where the thing was.

A long tongue flickered out from between its needle teeth. Tasting the air?

Then it erupted into motion and raced out of view, too fast for her to follow it with the lamp. Lana steeled herself and aimed the lamp downwards.

She was not given to screaming, but this was a nightmare, a horror. This looked like oncoming death.

A swarm of the things raced up the slope towards the ledge on which she stood. They were fast. Blind, yet they could feel her, smell her, hear her, read her mind. They knew that she was there and they were coming for her.

Lana ran. Her cry of fear, now a warning. She hauled the projectile weapon from her belt holster. She didn't want to hurt these things. They might be sentient. They might be pure animal. Whichever it was, she had to assume the worst.

She saw Kris, half-turned, frozen, weapon drawn. She was momentarily dazzled by his suit lamps then she saw his fear.

No, Kris. Don't.

"No –"

They fired. The bullet whip-cracked past Lana's head as she dived to the floor. There was a pig-squeal from behind. Lana used her momentum to surge back onto her feet. She turned and saw the bloody wreckage of the first of the creatures.

She also saw more of them, further off but coming on fast.

Ahead of her, Kris was still down on one knee, pistol raised, right hand steadied by their left.

"Run," she shouted. "Don't kill any more of them. Just run."

As she followed Kris, Lana glanced back and saw the other arachnids hesitate. Her last glimpse was of them scuttling about their dead. They looked for all the world as if they were sniffing at it, running their long legs delicately over the creature. They seemed puzzled, uncomprehending.

Lana was certain that they weren't going to mourn for long. If they had any level of intelligence, they would be out for revenge. If they were creatures of instinct, they would resume the pursuit. The more distance she and Kris could put between themselves and the arachnids the better.

Kris was quick, light on his feet and fit. Lana had also kept herself in shape but was bruised and exhausted. The heavy parka and the breathing mask made it hard to maintain a fast pace.

She heard the sound of their multiple scrabbling feet but didn't look back. They were closing on her. She was finished. She drove herself on, gasping for breath.

"Lana, Lana."

She saw them. Kris, standing in the tunnel's exit. They held out their hand. Lana surged forward, concentrated on their hand and only their hand. She wasn't going to make it. She wasn't going to make it –

Kris's hand closed about hers and they yanked her forwards. The two of them lurched out of the tunnel and back into the entrance cave then sprinted towards its entrance. Lana looked back.

Two of the creatures raced out of the tunnel. They hesitated a moment, tongues flickering.

"No eyes. They're adapted for the dark," Lana said. "Hopefully they won't follow us out –"

The first of them reared then leapt towards them. Lana saw Kris scramble out of the cave and onto the rock fall. Lana was hard on their heels. Her right boot came down onto the jumble of boulders. Something gave way and she tumbled sideways and rolled. Her lamp gave her glimpses of rock and mountain and sky then rock again. The world was a painful stroboscopic madness.

The fall ended. She lay still for a moment while she struggled to get air into her lungs. She realised that the life support pack was broken. She moved her fingers and toes, then her legs and arms. Finally, she sat up. At least her bones were intact.

She heard Kris, calling to her through the commer, asking her if she was okay.

"Yeah, yeah, I'm fine." She wasn't. "No air supply, more bruises, but that's all." She looked around, wildly, panicked.

No sign of the creatures. Kris's question was answered. It didn't appear that the creatures left the caves. Probably too cold out here, or they were sensitive to the radiation. Well, that was one good thing.

Lana ordered Kris to go on ahead, but they insisted on staying with her. She was glad of their company. With no life-support pack, she was going to have to take the journey more slowly. Lana was consumed by loneliness despite their presence. She wasn't afraid, instead the intense dark brought with it a deep melancholy. The tiny, ever-moving world created by her lamps, was surrounded by nothing. This planet was surrounded by nothing. The whole universe was nothing.

As Lana and Kris picked their way carefully back

towards the archway and the camp, Lana became
convinced that they were being followed. She was sure
she could hear the scrabbling of multiple claws. Her
imagination, of course it was, but the sensation filled the
darkness. She was afraid, but also resigned. There was
nothing she could do about it. She couldn't run. The
battering she had taken during her fall, shortness of
breath due to the thin cold air, combined with the brutal
crash landing she had endured, were taking their toll on
her and she struggled to walk now.

*

"I know," Isabella said. "I know why we are here."

"They told you?" Chien said. The hangar control room
was silent now, and still. Even the sounds of the *Drake's*
lingering demise couldn't disturb the peace in here. They
both knew that they would have to face the journey to the
seed module soon, but at that moment neither were in a
fit state to make the attempt.

"No," Isabella said. "No, I felt it. That moment, when I
was on the floor. When they healed me. We
were...*joined*. I was part of them..."

It had taken a while for the chaos in her mind to clear
and for her to be able to make sense of what she had
learned. The contact had the quality of a dream. It was
terrifying, a multitude of voices clamouring in her head.
Many and yet one. The Iaens were not physical beings at
all, but energy, thought, existence, entities for whom time
meant nothing. They were already here, delicate,
filaments of their collective had long ago reached through
space and time to this point and beyond, which is how
they knew about the star and planet. Those ethereal
tendrils had been too fragile to survive, but the link had
been made.

The Iaens saw humankind as both allies and pack
animals, primitive and willing to please for a handful of
delicacies. Humankind were their means of travel, their
limbs and their tools. Human starships had become

carriers and spreaders of the Iaen collective; a passage outward in return for advanced technology such as the quantum drive, stasis tanks and self-repair. In this relationship, the Iaens were not possessors but riders, digging their spurs into their human mounts.

But there were many less complex sentient species in the universe, as well as other non-corporeal lifeforms, that *were* ripe for possession. Blinded by Iaen generosity, humankind had become the unwitting deliverers of a powerful and almost infinite soul-hungry demon to the far corners of the galaxy.

And now, through time itself.

The Iaens intended to establish an outpost, here at the end of things. One of myriads of staging posts that enabled their inexorable expansion not only through space, but through forever, all the while using humankind's restless outward urge as their host.

Isabella had also seen the missile that struck the *Drake*. A glimpse, but enough for her to recognise its human origin. Payment, perhaps, for the gift of bodily repair the Iaens had given to humankind and bestowed upon Isabella and her child. Whatever the reason, it was a murderous act committed to please a ruthless, manipulative ally.

"But it stops here, Chien," Isabella said. "Because I know the truth now and I will engineer the protos to be independent of them, to be noble, better humans than we are. They won't sell themselves to the Iaens, I promise."

*

"Are you okay, Kris?" Lana said.

The engineer had been quiet and withdrawn since they had returned from the cave.

The two of them were huddled in the dome, tired from a round of maintenance and checks on the surviving lander. The plan was to sleep for six hours then return to the *Drake* where they would download the information they had gathered on the planet's surface and its environment into the seed module's databank ready for Isabella to get to work on the protos, then bring them all home.

Home. Here.

Lana would be glad to get Chien and Isabella safely off the ship. There had been a comm from Chien, but the signal was too badly corrupted for it to make any sense. Lana hoped it hadn't been urgent. Or a cry for help.

Kris was at the hotplate, refilling their mug. "I panicked. Perhaps I could have waited a few moments longer. Those things were coming for us. We were trapped down there."

"You saved our lives," Lana said.

"Yeah. Maybe. But I killed a living thing that was simply protecting its home."

"Or looking for its next meal."

"Yeah, there is that. Doesn't make me feel any better though. Do you want more coffee?"

"No, thanks, and you'd better not be so generous with that. We don't have a lot of the real stuff left."

"I need the real stuff right now." Kris returned to his camp bed. "The worst part of this is the fact that we haven't changed. We're probably the last humans around, and what do we do? We kill. We were frightened, and we acted like primitives."

"Perhaps that's what we are now," Isabella said. "But you, we, didn't have much of a choice."

"I know. But what looked like aggression may have simply been the way we interpreted their actions. The Iaens were not known for their politeness, diplomacy or circumspection. Some of humankind's allies are…*were*…so alien that it was impossible to judge their mood or intent until it was made clear by communication."

"Unfortunately we don't have access to any of the linguists, behaviourists or diplomats that normally accompany first contact." Because they had long turned to dust. Lana sipped her coffee and it was the best drink she had experienced in her life. Another sip. "If it turns out that the arachnids are non-sentient, we need to consider them as a food source."

"We're vulnerable, you know that don't you, Lana. We don't stand a chance if those arachnids stage any sort of attack against us."

"Another reason to get the protos engineered and down here with us. Safety in numbers." War again. Defence, which would turn to attack. Conflict, always conflict. Kris was right about them returning to the primitive, except that humankind had never truly advanced beyond the ape defending its own territory and stealing it from others.

Later, sleepless and in need of solitude, Lana went back outside, fully kitted out this time with the spare life support kit. She walked away from the light spilled by the dome and lander complex, and out into the full dark. For once she relished its cocoon. She came to a halt at the edge of the ice lake and stared across to the horizon and the faint red tinge that separated the darkness of the lake from the darkness of the sky.

There was daylight over there. Lethal and unimaginably hot, but daylight, nonetheless.

Suddenly hating the darkness again, she headed back towards the dome.

And heard the sound. That familiar scuttling, chitinous claws on rock. She froze. Then spun about, breathing hard, glad of the oxygen rich mixture pumped out by the life support pack.

Shapes, glimpsed between the shadows further up the shore, then gone.

She ran, back towards the complex. Her boots slipped in the smooth folds of frozen lava. The parka was suddenly heavy and clumsy. When she reached the dome, she looked back into the dark. Nothing. It was out there though. Angry. Hungry. Moving in for the kill. Perhaps more than one. Dizzy, head spinning, Lana fumbled for the door pad. There. Hand open slammed down. Nothing. It took a moment. Too long.

The hatch slid open.

Inside.

Shouting for the floodlights to be activated, weapons taken up and armed.

The dome was strong, designed for harsh environments, but it wouldn't stand forever against a massed attack by monsters like the ones that lived here.

"It seems that they *can* leave the caves, after all," she said as she and Kris activated the dome's screen, to the vid feed from the complex's security cameras.

The shore was now bathed in harsh white light which gave view to petrified lava and the ice lake. The floodlights swept round to illuminate the surviving lander, first its landing feet, then the bulk of its hull. The light moved on to reveal the landward expanse of the shore and the wall of mountains beyond. Then back around to the shore again.

There it was.

The arachnid.

It waited, halfway between the complex and the ice lake. Its prehensile tongue flickered from its lipless mouth. Despite its invertebrate-like structure, there was something of the reptile about the creature's upper body, that armless torso and eyeless head.

"It's waiting," Lana said.

"It could be doing anything. We can't interpret its actions based on our own preconceptions, you know that as well as I do, Lana." There was genuine fear in Kris's voice.

"I'm going out to confront it."

"What? No, you can't. Lana, it's suicidal to go out there."

"We're wasting time hiding in here. We need to get to the *Drake*. But we need to know if there is another intelligent species here before we bring the protos back. I don't want to be responsible for a genocide. You both know as well as I do who usually comes off worst when races meet."

The indigenous, not the invader.

"We need to know so that Isabella can engineer some

tolerance into the protos. God, I don't even know if that's possible."

A moment. Stalemate. Lana's way outside blocked by Kris. Her determination to meet with the arachnid undiminished.

"Let me through, Kris. That's an order."

They relaxed a little. "I'm stepping aside under protest, commander."

"Noted," Lana said then replaced her thermal-respirator mask over her mouth and nose, pulled up the hood of her parka and opened the hatch.

The area immediately around the dome was still bright-lit by the floodlights, the arachnid was vivid and terrifying. It seemed unaffected by the light, which probably meant that it was completely blind. Lana wondered how it perceived the world around. Smell, sound, touch, perhaps a sonar mechanism like that used by bats on Earth.

Extinct now. Aeons gone.

The creature didn't change its posture as Lana approached. The only change was that the movement of its tongue quickened as if picking up some signal that emanated from her. Lana fought an urge to run. It grew harder to walk. She was closing in on the thing and was almost within striking distance. She kept her hands open and raised slightly from her sides. The arachnid probably couldn't see her but might pick up something from the gesture. Whatever heightened sense it possessed it would certainly know that she was terrified.

Carefully, she reached up to draw the hood from over her head. Then she moved her right hand to the zip and pulled it down. Finally, she removed the mask. She held her breath. The cold was instant and like plunging into the sea in mid-winter. It was knives that tore into her. It was pain in every joint.

She stood there, like that, until she was panting for breath and her lungs burned. She replaced the mask. Then, fingers and arms stiff, shivering so hard it was almost a convulsion, she re-closed the zip and drew the hood back over her head. The arachnid remained motionless throughout the whole performance.

She reached in the pocket and activated the commer's loudspeaker mode, needed because the mask would muffle any attempt at normal speech.

"I'm Lana," she said and pointed to herself. Her voice seemed lonely and bleak. "I command this mission."

The arachnid reared slightly higher, bringing the front pair of its legs off the ground. Lana tensed, waiting for the strike. For the violence, the pain and the oblivion that would follow it. She prayed that Kris wouldn't react to the change in the arachnid's posture. There was a sound, a harsh buzz, more vibration than voice. The creature was answering her. She threw back the hood and forgetting that the creature couldn't see her, nodded furiously and said "Yes, yes. You're talking to me. We're talking."

Another movement and something dropped to the ice from amidst the arachnid's tangle of forelegs. The creature scuttled back a short distance. It had left the object on the ground. Lana took a step forward to better see what it was. Fleshy, whiteish in colour. A segment of the fungus they had found in the cave. It was about the size of a human head.

A gift? Of food, perhaps?

Lana made to crouch down to take the offering.

And there was movement, fast, huge, violent. She fell back as the arachnid lashed in towards her, mouth wide open, buzzing furiously. In that moment it was the world. It was vast and horrific, and it was death. A trap. The fungus as bait. Here it came, an explosion of violence –

The arachnid snatched the fungus and reared. Another movement, as it twisted and threw the fungus back towards the ice. The segment landed on the rock behind the creature, who now scuttled around to take up what looked like a guarding stance.

Was it trying to tell her that the fungus was forbidden to her?

Of course, it could be playing, like a dog, but she doubted it. The arachnid was trying to communicate.

Perhaps it was trying to tell her, and the others, to leave their food supply alone. A long shot, it could be trying to tell her many other things as well. That they should fight for the food, or that the fungus was poisonous.

The last interpretation was undermined when the arachnid twisted about to take up the fungus again then rammed it into its own mouth. It appeared to swallow the food whole. A moment later, the creature dropped onto its normal-belly down posture and scuttled away along the beach through the outer edge of the search light field and away into the darkness. No invitation to follow. No further message. Gone.

Exhausted and startled to still be alive, Lana headed back towards the domicile.

*

A sound broke into Isabella's dreams and woke her. For a moment she couldn't remember where she was. Exhausted she struggled to comprehend what the noise might be. She needed to rest, to sleep, but the bleeping and blaring would not let go. She felt light-headed. It was growing cold. She curled herself more tightly. Something was wrong. She wasn't in her bunk but sitting up, cramped, uncomfortable.

The flight control cabin, that's where she was and something was badly wrong.

Chien was here with her. Asleep on the floor, leaning against the window.

"...life support failure...module...warning, life support failure in hangar module...warning..."

It was growing hard to breathe, but she wasn't sure that she cared.

"Warning, life support failure in hangar module..."

Warning.

Warning.

Warning.

She started. Oh Jesu, they had to get out of here. She struggled out of the chair then grabbed at Chien and shook him as hard as she could. He mumbled then opened his eyes Breathing had become a battle. Isabella righted herself, gathered what strength she had and lurched across the room to the emergency EVA suit that hung along the back bulkhead.

She lifted it from its hook.

"Chi? Hurry."

"No...No, you're needed...the protos. There are more suits out in the corridor."

"Please Chi."

"Get the fucking suit on, Bella. Now!"

She knew he was right.

She began the struggle. The suit seemed stiff and awkward. She couldn't remember how to draw it up over her legs and torso. The fixings were too tight and difficult. She stopped, fought her panic down to a manageable level and pushed her arms into the sleeves. A twist and wrestle but she had it on. There was almost no air. She hauled breath into her lungs. She was light-headed. Grey mist swam across her vision.

Chien, where was he?

There, standing, leaning against the glass viewing wall. His arms were tight about himself. He shivered and was obviously disorientated by oxygen deprivation.

She picked up the helmet that weighed many tons and almost dropped it into place. Her fingers seemed to have lost all feeling and were no longer under her control. She wanted to kneel. Her legs were about to give way. A slight twist, clamps in place, sealed tight.

Suffocating now, trapped inside her suit. She panicked, grabbed at the helmet clamps then remembered. There was a switch. On her arm. There. There. She jabbed at it with her gloved hand which was too big and numb. Darkness crept in from the periphery of her vision.

A final jab. She heard a hiss then there was air.

Isabella breathed hard and allowed herself a few moments to experience the sheer joy of breathing then pulled the air pipe from the helmet and passed it to Chien. They could share oxygen until they could get to the nearest of the emergency suits. If only the air pressure could hold at a survivable level long enough.

Chien was on his feet and trembling violently. The temperature had already plummeted.

Air hose re-attached, Isabella took a handful of deep breaths as they made for the door, then it was Chien's turn again. They didn't have much time.

Out in the corridor now, moving as fast as they could towards the nearest exit hatch. Chien grew weaker. She had to drag him. Her arm was about his shoulders to keep him on his feet. The act was made cumbersome by the suit. There, a few metres and they would reach the suits hanging from their quick-snatch brackets by the hatch.

A few metres.

A few miles. Isabella's turn to breathe. Chien's. Isabella was forced to disconnect and re-attach the hose now. Chien's hands were too cold and stiff. His fingertips were blackening.

She grabbed at a suit. Chien slumped against the wall then slid down to the floor and sank onto his side. He no longer shivered. His lips were cyanosed. Shouting at him to wake up, crying and angry, Isabella tried to lift one of his legs into the suit. He wouldn't help her. He wouldn't cooperate. He wouldn't wake up and look at her.

He wouldn't breathe.

She wrestled at the tangled suit until she was able to activate its life support then tried to get the hose into his open mouth. Nothing. No response.

He stared at her, eyes wide and unblinking.

Ice had formed on his blue-tinted skin.

He wouldn't breathe. Why wouldn't he breathe? Please God, make him breathe…

Isabella knew the truth. She understood the truth, but she couldn't accept it.

She slumped to the floor and shuffled her suit-clad legs under him until she could rest his head in her lap. She stroked his hair, too numb to weep, too shocked to think or take any action other than this one tenderness.

Chien was dead.

Her Chien, her lover, was dead.

The Iaens. Why weren't they helping her?

"Where are you?" she whispered. "Where are you? Help him. Please. Bring him back. Bring him back bring him back bring him back…"

There would be no resurrection this time because the Iaens had gone.

Isabella's heart broke and she howled out the pain, which would never leave her.

*

"It attempted to communicate. They are sentient and they are concerned that we could seriously deplete their food source." Lana was still shaken from the encounter. "Perhaps, they'll leave us alone if we stay out of their caves."

"That's a hell of a lot of assumptions, Lana."

"It talked to me, it showed me what it wanted from us."

"Okay, suppose it did," Kris said. "But will we leave them alone?"

"We have no reason to disturb them again."

"You're right, we don't. But we intend to bring the seeds of a new civilisation down here. But you know, as well as I do, that humans don't share."

"It doesn't have to be that way."

"I can't see how it won't."

"We control the protos," Lana said. "We programme them to be what we want them to be."

"It's not an exact science," Kris said. "We're not gods. We're not producing robots here. They'll possess free will and have personality traits we can't predict. The raw material is cloned from humans like you and I."

"What are you trying to say?" Lana snapped out the question. Weariness and stress were not conducive to patience. "That we don't bring the protos down here. That we die out and leave Isabella's child alone here for much of its adult life?"

"No. Of course not. We don't have much choice on that matter now. I guess I'm playing Devil's Advocate, but there is something that we haven't considered," Kris said.

"Which is?"

"It's unlikely that the arachnids have finished with us. That they haven't simply scuttled off to their caves and will leave us alone from now on? You said it yourself, Lana, the protos may have to defend themselves, we have to programme that in."

"Defence, not aggression." Christ, we're being naïve, Lana added silently. "This could be a new Eden for humankind."

"Yes, it could. But remember that every Eden has its serpent."

"We can teach them," Lana said. "They'll have technology and knowledge that Adam and Eve never had or could dream of."

"And we'll make a better fist of it than God Himself, will we?"

"We launch in two hours, as planned." Lana didn't want to take the argument any further because she was not sure that she could win. "When the *Drake* will be at its closest."

*

Isabella walked. She felt no emotion now. Her mind was glass-clear and razor-edged with rage. She walked because she was unwilling to risk the transport tube. Hurtling around the rim of the Drake would take her through some of the most badly damaged areas. She had visions of the capsule, with her, inside, hurtling out of some broken section of the tube and into space. She didn't care about the pain that would cause, or the horror of waiting to die out in the solid black. But she did care about achieving her goal. She did care about the child growing in her womb. She did care about engineering all traces of the Iaens out of the protos and creating a new Eden down on the planet's surface. These were the reasons she needed to stay alive.

At first the trek along the main corridor was uneventful.

Other than areas of scarring from the original collision and self-repair, there was little to indicate that there was anything wrong with the star ship. Isabella knew, however, that to remove her helmet would mean instant death. The life support system was failing throughout the vessel now. She plundered two spare air-supply packs from other emergency EVA suits on the way, to ensure she had enough time to complete her task.

The vid screens that remained operational at each node station along the way, gave views of the red sun, close, vast, and reaching out to enfold the *Drake* in its gravitational embrace.

Then came the first disaster area.

Just beyond engineering lay a stretch of ruin that had once been a corridor. The surviving superstructure formed an open ribcage to which tattered scraps of the steel walls still clung. The righthand ribs were momentarily bloodied by the light of the vast sun, seen as a fiery dome that slid dizzily across the blackness as the Drake tumbled. Isabella stood in the open hatch. The route through this dereliction was hazardous.

The ship's gravity hub was still in place, and that made the journey to the far hatch even more dangerous. Isabella was forced to clamber over the torn sections of hull that littered what was left of the floor. At least there was light. The colour of blood, yes, but light, nonetheless. Trying to negotiate this deadly obstacle course in the pitch darkness with only the beam of a helmet lamp for illumination would have been unthinkable.

Isabella stumbled to a halt.

The floor was gone.

She teetered on the shattered edge and looked down into blackness.

Most of the lower sections of the ribs were intact and formed rungs over which she could climb, except that they were too far apart for her to reach. The longitudinal spar that joined them together was broken near its mid-point, which meant that she couldn't use it as a tightrope. She gripped the nearest of the verticals and tried to think.

She was breathing too hard. The suit's recycling system no longer outstripped the air supply reservoir. Isabella needed to stop, rest and let her respiration rate slow. But there wasn't time. The vibrations she could feel through her feet and hands were clear indications of the *Drake's* structural distress.

Isabella spotted a length of broken inner hull skin. Long enough to provide a bridge between ribs. She could drag it into position and begin the laborious process of climbing over the bottomless pit to the relative safety of the fragment of intact floor in front of the far hatch.

Isabella dropped to her hands and knees and pushed the hull shard forwards towards the first rib. As the length extended over space the lever effect made it increasingly difficult to hold onto the metal. She wrestled it into position, then set off across the makeshift bridge on her hands and knees.

She crawled over the abyss.

She concentrated on the metal. It was a metre wide at its broadest, less than a metre at its narrowest. It shifted as she crawled. She tried to look up at where she was going but the darkness below drew her attention. She caught herself gazing down at the wire struts that met at the gravity hub, visible in the planet-reflected sunlight. She noted that some of them had snapped and trailed behind the ship as it tumbled through its orbit of the planet. The only sound was her own hard breathing, made tremulous by fear.

A moment of dizziness. She grabbed the edges of the bridge and closed her eyes, willing herself not to overbalance. If she fell the gravity hub would snatch her. The wires would slice her to shreds on the way down.

She continued her journey and made it to the first of the ribs. Now came the awkward business of setting herself astride the rib, hauling the metal across to the next one. Her arms shook from the effort. Her legs ached from holding her in place.

The bridge dropped into place. Isabella took a breath and set off once again.

*

The launch was rough. The lander seemed cumbersome, its controls sluggish. It yawed alarmingly to the right as it lifted off. Kris swore loudly as they fought the controls. For a moment, as the lander slid sideways, they wondered if it was all over, but they were, as Chien had said, a good pilot and managed to level the craft then send it hurtling over the frozen sea towards the sun-bloodied horizon.

They wrenched its nose upwards.

And hit the launch thrusters.

They were slammed back in their seat, crushed into its embrace. Their heart laboured as a thousand tonne weight bore down on their chest. The lander bucked, kicked and shuddered. The thrusters' roar, though muffled, filled the cabin and added to the terror. On their back now, face to the black, lightless sky, Kris wondered why human beings continued to leave then re-enter the atmospheres of both their home and other planets after what must have been that nightmarish first space flight. This was hell. It was always hell.

But all launches were short lived and suddenly the sound died and smoothed out and they were in space. Weightless, their body now pressed upwards against the straps. Kris glanced out the port and saw the arc of the planet. It was dark and limned by the glare of its sun, which was still hidden below the horizon. Then the planet dropped away, and they saw the *Drake*.

It was a heart-breaking sight.

A dying starship, plunging around the planet in ever-lower orbit.

The repairs it had made to itself were coming apart. The self-repair function was never meant for such cataclysmic disasters as the one that had befallen the *Drake*. In linear flight through empty – and God, it really was empty – space, the stresses were not enough to cause damage, but the strain of ion drive deceleration, and its present fight against gravity, had burst its stitches and it was bleeding to death.

Debris spilled from its wounds like blood. Its stabilising thrusters obviously defunct, the vessel tumbled rim-over-rim through its final journey. There were lights on, in the control module, the hangar, and the seed module. A few lights twinkled on the hull, but huge areas of the ship were now dark. As they brought the lander round for an approach, Kris saw a huge hole where the patched-up hull had broken away. Large pieces of the *Drake's* skin cartwheeled about the vessel to create a deadly obstacle course.

"We'll have to match its spin," Kris said to Lana who was buckled into the seat behind them. "The gees will be unpleasant, so prepare yourself."

Kris brought the lander closer. The *Drake* was now an immense hammer that swung down towards them, each half of the rim narrowly missing the lander's nose cone as it slammed through its cycle. Their former home had become a terrifying, monstrous weapon.

Kris glanced back at Lana, who gave the appearance of calm, but that could mean anything.

Kris swung the lander to the right, away from the oncoming *Drake* then back to the left so that they were aimed at the axis of its spin. They punched in the steering jets and threw the lander into a spin of its own. As the first rotation began, they fired a lateral jet to push them into a sideways spiral motion. For a moment Kris saw the docking arm, extended and ready to receive them. Its locking port resembled an open hand. It arced away to the left. More spin, more lateral motion. Lana groaned behind them. The gees were vice-like. It was hard to breathe.

A huge irregular slab of metal spiralled into view. Kris saw rivets, a serial number. Scarlet sunlight swept over the curved, battered surface of the fragment as it filled the forward window. They fired the dorsal jet, broke out of the spin. The lander leapt over the fragment. The planet lurched into view. The *Drake* spun out of view.

Sweating now, muscles aching, Kris brought the lander round and made another approach, once again setting up a high-gee spiralling rotation, then slowing it to synchronise with the star ship. They felt sick. The increased gravity pressed on their chest and shortened their breath.

The locking port slid into the centre of the screen. It rotated slowly, then slower until the motion of the two vessels matched and it was motionless. Kris brought the lander in, slowly, slowly, gently, retros firing.

Closer now. Something clanged against the lander's hull and, once again the port juddered out of sight. Kris rammed the reverse thrusters into life and the *Drake* moved back.

A third approach. Small debris raced across the gap between the lander and the locking port. In, closer. Closer. Closer. The nauseating cycle of the planet ignored now. Lana silent. No breath.

Closer.

Closer. Slightly right, then left. Closer.

Then a thud and shudder. Servos whined; the sound transferred through conduction into the lander. The docking clamps locked then the arm swung the lander round to secure it against the *Drake's* airlock.

*

"Helmets on, visors sealed. Extra life support packs. We can't guarantee air in there."

The airlock hatch opened. Lana was first in. They had returned to the *Drake*.

But it no longer felt like home.

There was no light in this section. Lana found its absence even more claustrophobic than the caves down on the planet's surface. She was tired of the dance of suit lamps, of the swirling blackness. The imaginings.

The airlock opened into a node which housed one of the secondary control stations built at regular intervals around the ship's rim. This place was a ruin. There had been a fire. The suit lamps revealed scorched walls, shattered instruments and the tangled looms of cable, their insulation melted away.

The hatch hung open, its paint blistered and scorched. Lana led the way out into the corridor beyond. More fire damage, although it faded as they put distance between themselves and the node.

At least there was some illumination here. Sections of the corridor lighting still worked, fed by the ship's radiative generators. The going was hazardous however, panels had broken loose from the walls and were scattered over the corridor floor. The crew were constantly forced to weave and duck. Sharp edges meant torn suits.

And all the time, Lana commed Isabella and Chien. There was silence. No reply. Nothing.

They walked on. Parts of the corridor were intact and bright-lit, other sections darkened and in ruins. They stumbled to a halt when they passed through a bulkhead isolation hatch to find a gaping hole in the floor and roof of the corridor beyond. A string of LEDs hung like the strands of a spider's web. There was enough floor left by one of the walls for them to shuffle past the hole to the next hatch. As they worked their way from pipe bracket to pipe bracket, Lana looked down to see the planet race past. Her stomach heaved and she was almost sick. It passed by several more times before she reached solid floor again.

They reached the engineering module. A flickering light washed workbenches and maintenance equipment in irregular stroboscopic madness.

Lana was sure that they were not alone. She resisted the urge to look back. She heard whispering, then realised that it was Isabella, her voice soft in the comm.

"Isabella? Isabella, its Lana. Where are you?"

"I'm in the seed module." She sounded oddly cold. "Are you on the ship?"

"Yes, we're on our way. Is Chien with you?"

"He's dead." No emotion. No tears, only that icy calm. "Be careful, commander, there are gaps and holes everywhere. I only just made it."

"I'm so sorry. Isabella are you okay –"

"The Iaens are behind all this."

"The Iaens?" Humankind's closest ally? "Isabella, what are you saying?"

"They're using us. They've been using us since our first contact with them."

"How do you know this? What happened?"

"They were on the ship."

The comm was cut.

"Did you hear that, Kris?"

"Yes. I never believed the Iaens to be angels, but this?"

For a moment, as they moved on, Lana yearned for the *Drake's* final plunge so that its death agonies would be over. She had always felt that modern starships possessed a certain level of sentience, that the sheer complexity of their systems imbued them with something resembling life. And the *Drake* certainly did feel as if it was alive.

Deeper. Through storage tunnels where cables hung from broken ducts and conduits. There was a hole. No air to suck them out, however. It had long been distributed into the emptiness outside.

On, into a lit area. Closer to the seed module now.

There was another fracture here, a hole ripped into the walls, surrounded by a set of puncture wounds. Liquid dripped from broken pipes. A panel lamp flashed on and off.

Hatch open, through the link tube then the far hatch and into the seed module.

Here, then was the future of humankind.

*

Let them sleep, Lana said silently as she crossed to the engineering station where Isabella waited. Let them rest, unaware and un-alive.

The two women managed a clumsy, EVA suit embrace. Lana wanted to give some wise comfort to the bereaved comms officer but could think of nothing to say. Instead, she handed over the data drive that held the necessary environmental information Isabella needed to get to work.

"There's a life form on the planet," Lana said. "I believe it to be sentient. There seems to be no sophisticated civilisation down there, but one of their number did attempt communication. You need to factor that into the data feed. Tolerance, but also willingness to defend themselves."

"It's not that easy," Isabella said. "I'll do what I can. The protos are human at their core. I can develop the necessary physical attributes. I can enter race memory and knowledge, but their souls... That is out of my hands."

Kris stayed to assist Isabella, while Lana went forward to prepare the module for launch and planetfall. She found that she missed Kris's presence. Their time together on the planet's surface, brief as it was, had begun to transform Lana's feelings for the engineer into something that might be love. It was certainly a need for closeness.

Lana trudged up the metal steps to the top gantry. The suit was heavy, the shifting gravity, caused by the *Drake's* erratic tumble, made movement awkward and exhausting. Once in the module's control station, she dropped gratefully into the seat and took a moment to catch her breath.

Kris's voice in her helmet. "Are you sure you should be the one bringing the module to the surface, Lana?"

"You're the engineer, you're needed down there. So is Isabella. I'd rather she was in *your* hands for the descent. These protos are expendable. You're not."

"We'll be lucky if any of us make it through the *Drake's* debris field."

"We'll be lucky, Kris."

"And, Lana, *you're* not expendable."

Test protocols complete, with all systems go for flight and descent, Lana returned to the others. She watched Isabella at the genetic engineering station, and wondered what this was for. Again, she had questioned their fulfilment of their mission in these changed and alien circumstances. Yes, they would keep the spark of humankind glinting in the dark. Yes, they were propagating their race, and wasn't that the most urgent imperative of any living organism?

What had come to trouble her most was Isabella's claim that the Iaens had been on the *Drake* and were behind the fake collision and the deaths of nearly all the ships' crew. The Iaens, who had condemned the four chosen survivors to live out their lives in the dark in the shadowlands of an inhospitable planet far, far from home, both spatially and temporally.

All to establish an outpost here at the end of time.

It made no sense because the Iaens had been benevolent to humankind since their first encounter.

So benevolent they had murdered twenty souls.

The *Drake* shuddered.

There was an immense explosion from somewhere distant. Unheard in the vacuum. But felt as its shock wave ripped through the ship's hull and superstructure and caused a minor earthquake that almost knocked Lana from her feet. There was something ominous about that blast.

The lights dimmed, returned then flickered and dimmed again.

There was a sensation that the ship's trajectory had changed.

Illusion, surely. But a persistent one, nonetheless.

Then came another explosion. This one felt much closer. The vessel trembled. A huge object thudded against the hull. Another and another. The impacts were loud and terrifying.

The *Drake* was breaking up.

Kris was on their feet again. "We have to get back to the lander."

More impacts and explosions. Lana doubted that the lander still existed. Kris staggered across to the module's vid screen, which remained stubbornly blank until, suddenly, there were images of debris and ruin. The camera gave a view along the hull towards the *Drake's* forward section. Flame boiled briefly from a gaping wound, a hundred or so metres ahead. The area around it bled debris. Something immense tumbled away into space, a vast section of the ship, quickly swallowed by the darkness. The planet swung into view. Kris moved to other cameras.

There it was. The docking port.

The lander resembled a vulnerable toy, clinging to the arrester arm, which had become unattached from the airlock and now swung limply out into space.

Then all Lana could see was the planet as it once again flashed dizzyingly past. It looked bigger. Closer.

They were dropping fast, destined to hit the atmosphere at ninety degrees, which meant that the *Drake* would be reduced to molten slag long before it hit the surface.

*

Isabella worked her fingers through the complex virtual webbing that was the fibrous weave of the protos' essence. She threaded and knitted and sewed their lives into place using patterns that had been imprinted into her brain hours before the mission commenced. There had been six crew members who had been given the same data stream. Only she survived. The responsibility was hers.

She was sick with the effort. The pattern was infinitely complex, every thread, every knot every twist had to be exact. She became conscious of her name being spoken.

"Bella?"

Chien, he was here?

She wanted to look up. She wanted to see him.

No.

He was dead. He was gone. She must keeping working.

"Isabella." It was Lana. "We've run out of time. We have to go. Now."

Isabella shook her head, the slightest movement. She was close now.

Low oxygen requirements. Large chest and lungs. Large heart. Fast metabolism. Able to function in low oxygen conditions. High body temperature, able to survive in the extreme cold. Tall, stronger than basic humans, fast. Powerful beings capable of living on a harsh world. No need for human vision, but ability to see on different frequencies. It was all in the weave of the fabric, each thread, each movement transferred into the proto tanks. Isabella's fingers weaved the reflection of their actual matter. She built them. She needed a little more time.

She felt Kris's hand on her shoulder and gently shrugged them off. She would not leave this ship without the protos. Her child would not spend the last phases of its life alone.

The final threads now. The final twists and plait.

The *Drake* shuddered and convulsed. Isabella hung on, keeping her hands steady by sheer force of will.

"Isabella, come on. Isabella, please."

"It's done. We have to go." Lana this time.

She was right. The last thread, strung from node to node. The image flared then dissolved. And then the lights burned brightly in the pods as the protos began to form according to her design.

*

Another explosion threw Lana onto her back. She saw Kris stagger and grab at Isabella.

"Lana?"

"I'm okay. Go, Kris, get out of here. I'm fine. *Go*."

Lana heard their voice in her helmet commer. "I love you."

Then Kris and Isabella were gone, on their way to the lander.

Blanking out any emotion she felt, Lana set off for the module's command station.

*

Kris and Isabella manoeuvred awkwardly through the swirl of debris. The *Drake* tumbled faster now. It was impossible to stand, so they crawled. The violent motion made Kris feel sick. They were disorientated, unsure whether they were traversing the floor, wall or ceiling.

The ship trembled. Whole sections of hull were gone. Kris and Isabella hauled themselves over the rib struts, trying not to be distracted by the dizzyingly fast passage of the planet across their line of vision.

They reached a point at which there was mostly space. To the right and left and below. One piece of hull remained intact and formed a bridge over the gap. Kris watched Isabella crawl onto it then followed. They gripped its sides, clinging on as they fought the centrifugal effect that sought to throw them into the void.

When Isabella reached the far side she commed Kris to follow her out onto the Drake's hull. It was a good idea. The ship's interior was becoming increasingly difficult to negotiate and at any moment they might find it impassable. Dangerous as it was, travelling on its exterior would be faster. Isabella clambered out through the broken hull. Kris crawled in her wake and grabbed at any handhold they could find.

Debris pattered against Kris's EVA suit. They prayed that nothing would pierce the fabric. They clung on as centrifugal force tugged at them, seeking to hurl them into space. The planet was a vast wall that flew by and felt as if it was about to consume them.

Isabella and Kris slithered over the Drake's outer skin one handhold at a time. They were almost too weary to carry on, but to rest meant certain death.

And there was the lander. Swinging in a lethal arc at the end of the docking arm. Surely impossible to reach.

"We crawl," Isabella said. The cold determination in her voice chilled Kris to their soul. It was purpose, driven by fury. Kris wondered if Isabella would ever recover or remain broken and consumed by that rage for the rest of her life.

"We use the lanyards do you understand me?" Kris said. "And we hang on because our lives fucking depend on it."

This time Kris went first and led the way down the handholds to the airlock then across the docking port towards the joint where the arm met the hull. The journey was made painstaking by the clipping and un-clipping of their lanyard clamps.

Concentrate on the hull, on what's in front of you. Hold on and fight the centrifugal force. Don't look outwards, at the blackness, or at the mad arc of the planet.

There was a maintenance ladder clamped to the side of the docking arm joint. The climb was hard. Both Kris and Isabella were nearing absolute exhaustion. But up they went. Hand-over-hand, boots finding each rung. One more pull. One more effort. Until they stood atop the joint, watching the docking arm swing back and forth, dragging the lander with it. The top surface of the arm was about two metres below them, and two metres wide. There was a handrail along one edge, there for the safety of any engineers who might have to walk its length.

"We pick our moment," Isabella sounded matter-of-fact, as if this was mere routine. "Then we jump."

And break an ankle or worse. Or misjudge the moment or angle and get thrown off into space, either hurled far enough outwards to be snatched into everlasting darkness by zero-g or bounced over the side to fall and shatter against the ship's gravity core.

Isabella took Kris's hand. The two of them stood together on the top of the joint and watched the arm swing back in from their right. It came in fast. This was impossible. This couldn't be done. This was –

"Now!"

Isabella jumped and took Kris with her. For a moment they fell through absolute nothingness.

Their boots slammed into the top of the arm. Instinctively, Kris let their legs bend to absorb the shock then dived forwards onto their hands. The safety rail…Kris grabbed blindly to the right and found the rail then snapped on the lanyard clamp.

Isabella. She wasn't there. Christ, she had missed. She was gone –

Kris spun round and saw her, clinging to the safety rail, scrabbling at it with her lanyard clamp. Kris moved carefully back to her and steadied her hand so that she could clamp on.

There remained now the slow careful walk over the wildly swinging arm to the lander. Perilous, yes, but at least they had the safety rail to cling to and lanyards to tether them in place.

As they progressed, the influence of the ship's gravity sphere steadily diminished, until they were weightless. Their feet left the arm's surface, forcing them to travel hand-over-hand along the rail, torsos and legs floating behind.

Close now.

Something broke. Kris felt a tremor and the lander was wrenched away from them. The docking port was breaking up. Another shudder and Kris was jolted off the arm and into space. They tumbled over and over, wildly grabbing at nothing, until the lanyard jerked them back. They activated the spool and flew up to the rapidly dissolving docking arm where they grabbed the rail and hung on. They saw debris bleeding from the union between the docking port and the lander. A bad sign.

"Isabella, hurry. The lander's breaking loose."

Kris felt her hand on their shoulder. "Here, I'm here."

"We have to detach at the last moment and take a leap. Are you okay for that, Isabella?"

"Are *you*?"

"About as ready as you are," they said. "Let's get as close as we can."

Another approach to the lander, which flapped dangerously at the end of the broken arm. It looked to Kris as if it would snap off and be hurled clear at any moment. It swung outwards then back and there was a moment when the hatch was in clear view.

"Now!"

"You first, Kris –"

"No. Go. *Go*."

Isabella kicked against the safety rail, launched herself

off the arm. Kris saw her hurtle across the gap. She was too far to the left, Christ, she was going to miss. She reached out and Kris saw her grab at the handhold on edge of the hatch. She twisted about, palmed it open and swung herself inside.

"I'm in. Kris." Her voice, tight with fear, over the commer. "Kris hurry."

"Thank God."

"Your turn. Come on, please."

"I'll get it next time the lander comes past."

Kris tensed.

Ready. Ready. The lander was thrown to the left.

Then swung back towards him.

A few seconds.

It broke away.

Kris watched it flat-spin off into the dark, leaving a trail of wreckage behind it.

And experienced despair followed by an odd peace.

It was done. No hope now. It was over, but the final act would be on their own terms.

Kris unclipped the lanyard and fell backwards. A last glimpse of the lander, its drives ignited. The debris must have been from the docking port and not the craft, thank God. Then they closed their eyes and whispered "Lana, I love you," before reaching up to unlock their helmet catches.

*

Instruments indicated that the seed module was moving away from the *Drake*. Two metres... three metres... four... ten... Speed of clearance increasing.

Explosion.

The module skittered into a violent spin. Lana forced her thousand tonne arm outwards to activate the virtual controls. Thrusters fired. One failed. The planet raced across the vidscreen. Planet, space, planet space.

Lana closed her eyes to steady herself. She needed the thrusters to fire, stop the rotation and bring the module round to its re-entry course. She calculated then triggered the firing sequence.

The gees increased yet more. Lana struggled to breathe.

Then it eased.

The planet had steadied then disappeared as the module entered its nightside shadow. That thin red arc on its horizon was the only sign that the planet was there at all. Debris tumbled across the beams of the module's navigation lights. The *Drake* slid past to the right, horribly close.

"Lana, I love you." Kris's voice little more than a whisper over the commer.

"I love you too," Lana said.

No answer, only white noise. If they hadn't heard then she would repeat it when she saw them on the surface, over and over again.

More debris. A sideways slip to move out of the debris field.

The module's navigation systems found and locked on to the homing signal from the camp. The module manoeuvred itself into a re-entry arc.

Then, suddenly, there was a flare of light. The *Drake* reappeared in the vid screen, distant now and tumbling planet-wards, trailing its gravity hub behind, spewing debris from countless wounds. Its hull glowed cherry red then seemed to dissolve into a mass of fireballs that lit up the planet's atmosphere. In moments the titanic vessel had been transformed from solid object to a rain of burning wreckage.

Tears stung Lana's eyes.

It was an inanimate object.

It had been their home.

It had tried its best to protect them and complete its mission.

Ridiculous.

She couldn't help it. She couldn't fight what she felt.

Angle check. Too shallow. Thruster seven failed. The module began to tremble. Adjustment. Calculations in her head. This would have to be done on feel.

There, a glow and exhaust tail. The lander, ahead of her. They had made it, Isabella and Kris were on their way down.

She tipped the module into a steeper angle. It was dark now. Black. Everything was black. The black smothered her until it was lit by a hot ruby glow. The shaking grew worse, the vessel was airworthy but cumbersome and meant only for descent.

Alarms.

Thrusters failed. Threat of a spin.

Dizzy from the effort, Lana calculated, re-adjusted, fired off small thrusts to level up.

Then all was fire and the screams of the superheated airframe.

*

The lander careered surface-wards. There was flame and noise, but Isabella was oblivious to the hell of re-entry.

There was a truth that dug into her mind like a splinter. It was there and could not be denied. It consumed all her attention and focus. It was something she had learned from the Iaens during those moments of healing and oneness she had experienced after her near miscarriage.

Hadn't Lana told her that there was sentient life on this planet? Sentience but no evidence of civilisation. A tribal culture?

A primitive culture?

Hosts.

A foothold in this epoch to which the time and space spread (or was it infection) of the Iaens could anchor themselves.

But the Iaens in the starship were gone, dead, dissolved. No thread remained between now and the time at which the *Drake* was launched.

Yes, there was. Oh God, there was a foothold.

Because what was more primitive than an embryo, the living, yet unaware collection of cells that even now had its being in her womb? That moment, that instant when she and the Iaens were one, when her id, her soul, her *self* had been merged and melded with the Iaen collective, when the child within her was healed.

At that moment the child was no longer her own.

The protos, those new, near-perfect humans she had engineered, they would find a way to gulf the void between *then* and now. Guided, used, manipulated by her own son or daughter who was not her child at all but some human-Iaen hybrid. And what of the other race on the planet? To what use would they be put?

Re-entry ended with an abruptness that startled Isabella.

She wept now, for the loss of her baby, because *her* child was lost. Had the Iaens engineered the pregnancy and the miscarriage? Chien and Isabella, on the same mission because their psychological profiles suggested strong possibility of attraction, then driven together by the awfulness of their situation? Perhaps, the Iaens had counted on a mother's love for her unborn to blind her to the truth of what grew inside her.

They were right, that love was blind and all powerful, for her *own* child, but not for the disease that now infested her womb.

"Lander come in." Lana trying to make contact. "Lander, come in. Kris –"

"Kris is gone. They saved me. They were brave, but…"

There were mountains ahead of her, jagged peaks, sheer sides glimpsed in the lander's navigation lights. Isabella pushed the craft's nose down into a shallow dive. And as the loved are wont to do, she cried her lover's name in those last, brutal seconds of her life.

*

Then there could be no communication while the two craft plunged through the atmosphere, glowing, hot, shuddering so much it felt to Lana as if the module would break into pieces. Lana saw the lander. Ahead of her, a few metres, off to the left. A fireball, swinging into a lateral arc. Yawing. Barely under control.

She wanted to call out to Kris and Isabella. She wanted to shout their names and tell them that they would all be all right. Then the clouds broke, and the mountains appeared again. Humankind's new home for its ten-thousand-year twilight.

The madness passed. The module eased into horizontal flight, now turning as it followed the co-ordinates to the ice sea and the camp. There, the lander again. Too low. "Lander come in. Lander, come in. Kris –"

"Kris is gone. They saved me. They were brave, but…"

Gone? Dead?

The lander was too low.

Too low –

It collided with a mountain.

Quick, simple and clean. A billow of flame, a fountain of debris then a hundred burning fragments rolled down the smooth rock face like a fiery avalanche.

Nothing left.

Nothing could have survived.

There was only a rising column of smoke, black against the black and defined only by the reflected orange glow of burning wreckage below.

*

Kris…

She was alone on the surface. The module's landing had been perfect.

Locked in silence. No matter how loudly she screamed for someone to help her, to talk to her, there would be nothing but that soft static hiss from the commer.

There was no one.

No one.

No person, no voice, no touch.

No other human being in existence.

If Lana stripped naked and walked out onto the ice to freeze to death, no one would call to her to come back. No one would grab her and try to stop her. No one would know.

Kris, God...I can't lose you...

No one from the *Drake*. No one from Earth. No human in the entire universe.

So, what's it to be, Lana? Are you going to lie down and die? Is that how we end?

She could hear them, her lover and her friends. A question asked in their voices, each one quiet, measured, yet taut over the demons that fought for their souls.

Kris, this illusory Kris of the mind, was right. She could sit here in the seed module's command station, give in and let herself die, or she could prepare the way for the new Adam and Eve and their extended family. She could live among them and teach them what she knew and negotiate between them and the arachnids.

What did that make her, Lilith, God, or the serpent entwined about the Tree of the Knowledge of Good and Evil?

There was a glimmer of hope. The new humans, with their kickstarted knowledge and inbuilt technical acumen, might find a way to return her home, to her own place and her own time.

I want you to come back, Kris...Come back, please...

She needed to stop. They weren't coming back. Neither were Chien or Isabella. It was done, over.

That glimmer, that faint light in the black, was what hauled Lana from the control chair and back into the body of the seed module. She walked slowly along the central gantry between the pods, checking for failures, checking temperatures and staring in at the vaguely human shapes that had begun to form inside each one. The new humans looked to be taller than their creators, two, two-and-a-half metres. Muscular formation indicated strength and agility. Arms and legs disproportionably long, for climbing.

When is a human not a human?

The question flashed, unbidden into Lana's mind.

When the Iaens are involved, came the unwelcome answer.

They had been on the ship. They had been part of the

ship, melded into its weft and weave. These had not been the Iaens she had encountered throughout her career in the space faring business. They had been rough-hewn humanoid forms. Simulacrums, Isabella had called them. An acceptable face for god-like non-physical beings to show to lesser species.

They were humankind's allies.

Yet, even Lana who saw them as friends, had sensed something else. A coldness, a total lack of empathy, of compassion or emotion. The overwhelming feeling she had experienced had been *expedience*. Raw, brutal, need.

As she passed the final handful of pods, she began to wonder what they *actually* contained. Who were these beings? That question, again. When is a human not a human?

Then she was outside, on the ice. She still wore her EVA suit, which kept her warm. She drew on the helmet and closed the visor so she could breathe from its life support pack.

Here, on the shadow side of the module, cut off from the camp by its ungainly bulk, was that, now familiar, wall of blackness. It rushed in to smother her soul. That was where Lana broke and wept, helplessly, messily. She dropped to her knees and forced out their names; Isabella, who had loved Chien, and Kris who had loved her and whom she would have loved. There was also the nameless beginnings of Isabella's child.

Gone.

She stared across the lake to reassure herself that the planet's immense sun still burned in its sky. And yes, there was that blade of bloody light.

There were people out there on the ice too. Skating, of course, figures formed of night who sliced over the sea's frozen surface in complex weaving patterns. Lana raised her hand to wave and to get their attention.

Nothing. No one.

But ice, darkness and that bloody open wound between horizon and sky.

She spun about then walked along the module's flank,

under its wings, to its nose then onto the shore and up to the camp.

The systems in the module would take care of the protos. It would take at least three or four days for them to fully form, ready for their birth on the fifth day.

Exhausted now, she sealed the inside hatch of the dome's airlock, grabbed a ration pack and made coffee. She sat on her bed to eat and drink. Kris's possessions were neatly rolled on his camp bed, waiting for them to return. Their pack, parka and other items of personal kit were stacked by their bed. A hairbrush, a razor, a watch, a knife and fork, unwashed, lying inside a now empty ration pack. The ordinary. The poignant.

Kris was gone.

She would never know what that meant, but whatever sacrifice they had made for Isabella, it had been in vain because Isabella was dead. It had looked like suicide, but Lana could never know for certain.

It was when she ordered the lights to go off that Lana began to worry that Isabella might still be alive, huddled in the freezing darkness in the mountains where they had crashed. Isabella, injured, alone and frightened. She pushed back against the thoughts. But they wouldn't go away.

No one could have walked away, or even crawled from that crash.

The irrational thought had dug in its claws.

It followed her onto her dreams.

When she woke, a few short hours later, she knew that she had to be sure.

*

This was probably the last days she would be alone on the planet. By the time she returned to the complex, the protos would have hatched, been born, come to life. So, this expedition into the pitch black was, perhaps to be relished as much as endured. She had downloaded the crash co-ordinates from the seed module's navigation logs into a wrist-worn tracker.

Lana's world was reduced to the disc of white light cast by the lamp attached to her parka. She was aware of, but couldn't see, the mountains that loomed over her. She could feel their weight and overwhelming presence.

By the end of her first eight-hour trek, she was past the cave and the rock fall she and Kris had explored on that expedition away from the complex. The path they had followed snaked its way deep into the mountain range. It was rough and stony but walkable.

There were times when the darkness was close and almost unendurable, but Lana walked herself through the panic and claustrophobia.

On the second day, measured only by passage of time denoted on her wrist timer, she became aware that she was not alone. No hallucination this time. She could hear the scrabble of their claws. She heard the buzz of their communication. The arachnids were following her. She was sure that they surrounded her, and were moving in parallel, and that there were others up ahead.

She felt no threat from them. She felt no hostility. She was sure that they were curious.

She certainly posed no threat to them.

When she rested and ate, they paused too. She heard some of them move closer, but none ever entered the disc of light. It was movement, sound, and that sense one living thing has of another.

On the third day the path came to an end. There was a saddle shaped ridge ahead of her, that joined the flanks of two tall, slender, spire-like mountains. She increased the lamp strength and glimpsed their needle-like summits.

The saddle was a hard climb. The arachnids climbed it with her. She rested on its ridge, then moved slowly down its far side. The tracker bleeped loudly. She was close now. The exercise, the movement and purpose, vain as she knew it to be, exhilarated her. She felt at peace with the planet and its inhabitants.

When she woke from a short sleep, she found pieces of the fungus had been dropped onto the rock beside her. She picked up the smallest piece and ate. It had a meaty texture and taste. If it was toxic, then she was going to die here, far from home in the dark. She didn't care.

It satisfied her hunger. It also moved her to tears. The arachnids had fed her. They were trying, in their way, to show that they meant no harm and believed that she didn't either. At least, that was what she hoped they meant. Perhaps they were simply trying to poison her. The thought made her laugh.

On the third day she found wreckage. As she walked along the flank of the mountain, looking for more, she shone the lamps outwards and glimpsed the beginning of a desolate looking plain. She found more wreckage, unrecognisable, blackened, metal shards. Eventually it became a trail of debris. The fragments increased in size until she found what looked to be the remains of an engine. Lana found no bodies, but now knew for certain that Isabella would not have lived beyond that instant of fiery collision. Her ashes were scattered over the rocks, mingled with the dust.

Lana searched for rocks and began to pile them into a cairn.

Two of the arachnids joined in. She glimpsed them as shadowy, angular collections of legs and torsos that scuttered into brief view to each deposit large rock then disappear again.

Once it was done, she stood and remembered her crewmates. She allowed herself to weep one last time. Then turned away and set off back to the complex.

She made the return journey alone. No arachnids, no ghosts. Just the darkness and her memories and a sense that these two species of end-time beings had made some peace with each other.

*

It was the silence that woke her.

She was used to it now, but this was different. Lana sat up and activated the dome lamp. She was alone. She grabbed her mask and parka and went outside.

Two figures stood a few metres from the complex, caught in the glare of the security lights. Lana approached, carefully. They were tall and beautiful, but also disturbing. Their faces were finely formed, their features pronounced but perfectly balanced. Their ears were proportionally larger than standard humans but, in this environment, hearing was going to be an important sense. It was their eyes that unnerved Lana most. They were not human eyes, but white blanks. Sight was of little use here, she realised. Isabella had engineered them to see the world in a different way.

They were not alone. A dozen or so arachnids had gathered at the edge of the light. Lana sensed a vast number of them hidden it the darkness beyond. They were not moving. The two sentient species simply stood and stared at each other, whatever that meant to these eyeless beings.

A buzz of arachnid communication startled her. The new Adam and Eve did not respond or attempt communication. The arachnids tried again.

Still nothing from the new humans.

Until suddenly, Adam turned away and set off back towards the module. A few moments later, Eve followed. Adam passed Lana without saying a word. Eve paused, regarded her with an odd blind frankness, then pointed back towards the arachnids and said, "Primitives."

That single word chilled Lana to her soul.

Lana made to approach the arachnids herself, but those in the light backed away and faded into the blackness. She contemplated pursuing them and trying to explain but realised that it would be fruitless. And what was there to explain anyway? More aliens had come to the arachnids' world, and they were here to stay. It would be all right. They were enhanced, superior versions, intelligent, tolerant.

Except that they thought the native species *primitive*.

Feeling abandoned and unsettled, Lana returned to the dome.

She couldn't sleep.

Primitive.

The superior and the primitive did not mix. One would prevail. One would fall. Isabella's new humans were all but perfect. They needed no clothes. They could find their way around in the darkness. They possessed full knowledge and enough technology here on the landing site to begin the work of building a civilisation.

This planet was Eden to Adam and Eve and all the others like them growing to maturity in their seed tanks. Hell to Lana, but paradise to them. They would solve the quantum temporal jump riddle. They would travel time and take the technology back with them. They were an outpost here, in the far future.

They would not be the only ones to arrive on this planet. Humankind was driven by the outward urge, across their home world, through space, why not through time? The ape could not be caged. And with humankind would come their Iaen allies.

And what of the arachnids? The primitives for whom this was home?

If this really was a new Eden, then there would surely be a serpent.

Lana understood then what she had to do, and it would be terrible.

*

The wind was stronger now, blowing from deep in the dark side and across the ice towards its bloodied horizon. Lana sat down on the shore, unable to act. This was humankind's second chance. This was new humankind and yet history was again on the verge of repetition.

*

Lana headed up the ramp and into the bright-lit womb of the module. She hated the vessel now. It was suddenly a lumpy, ungainly mass cluttering this planet's surface. Artificiality slammed down onto the natural.

125

She went up to check that no more of the new humans had hatched. She walked along the central gantry. The tanks glowed bright but there was no movement from inside. She didn't look too hard at the shapes, but despite her studied disinterest, she knew that each one contained a thing of beauty, a work of genetic art.

There was no sign of Adam and Eve but they were here, somewhere in the maze of gantries. She hated the light in here as well. Odd, because she had been terrorised by the eternal darkness, now it seemed almost like home. This light was wrong. It was crass, an intrusion. A lie.

Movement. One of the new humans running along the gantry behind her, approaching fast.

Adam.

Lana reached into the pocket of her therma-coat and drew out the projectile handgun Kris had used in the cave. She couldn't remember putting it there. She must have known that she would need it when she left, the dome for this last task. She braced herself, raised the weapon, held it in both hands.

Adam was close. He was fast. He almost exploded out of the shadows and glare to fill the entire world with his perfection and beauty.

Lana fired, the detonation deafening and shocking. The weapon kicked in her hands. She felt the counter force of the blast push her back. She saw Adam thrown away from her. His mouth open. She saw an eruption of blood from his chest.

She heard a scream.

Eve.

Lana glanced to her left and down to see the woman clambering up the gantry. No need for stairs, she was agile, strong, and quick. Lana ran for the command module. She didn't look back. If she did, she would see Eve and she would falter. She gasped for breath, exhausted by shock rather than weariness. Another part of her was energised, driven by her purpose. There was fear in there as well.

She slammed against the control station hatch.

Feet pounded the gantry behind her. Eve, closing in.

Trembling, momentarily confused and unable to think or function, Lana leaned against the cold metal of the door and tried to remember how to get in.

Palm-pad. There. Palm-fucking-pad.

She slammed her hand onto the pad. The door opened. She stumbled through, spun about and as she palmed the door shut, glimpsed Eve.

The woman's mouth was open. She howled with what sounded like grief and rage. Lana wanted to let her in. Lana wanted to save her. But she couldn't. Not now.

The hatch slid shut.

Eve pounded the door. Dull thuds, beaten out with enough force to have broken a normal human's hand.

Lana slumped in the pilot's seat and opened the virtual controls. She pulled the visor over her eyes.

She scrolled through the commands until she found the one, she wanted.

Thud-thud-thud. The hatch shook in its frame. Lana was sure that the metal was bending inwards

Security?

"La8878."

Second security.

"M009t."

Self-destruct, final confirmation.

"La8878 and M009t, confirm."

Sequence initiated.

The pounding stopped. Eve must have finally quelled her rage enough to think. Would her palm work on the pad, or was she attempting to dismantle and override it? Lana wasn't going to find out. She was rose from the chair and launched herself at the emergency exit hatch.

Open. Ramp activated.

She rode it down, clung on. Hit the ice then ran.

She skidded and stumbled, out of breath.

Needed distance. Distance. Distance

Dis –

The darkness dissolved into a moment of brutal white.

Lana dived onto her belly. She saw the frozen lake, clear, smooth and seemingly infinite. A second later, the blast shattered the silence, its shockwave kicked her across the ice. Debris descended down in a rain of fiery fragments that smashed onto the lake, sizzled then darkened.

When it was done, Lana pushed herself back onto her feet and walked.

Humankind was gone. She was its murderer.

She was its end.

Ahead of her the planet's eternal day glowed fiery red. A destination she may probably never reach, and even if she did, the last star would kill her long before she reached the planet's noon meridian.

But, at least, she would die in the light.

ENDS

Elsewhen Press

delivering outstanding new talents in speculative fiction

Visit the Elsewhen Press website at elsewhen.press for the latest
information on all of our titles, authors and events; to read our blog;
find out where to buy our books and ebooks; or to place an order.

Sign up for the Elsewhen Press InFlight Newsletter at
elsewhen.press/newsletter

By Terry Grimwood from Elsewhen Press

INTERFERENCE

Terry Grimwood

The grubby dance of politics didn't end when we left the solar system, it followed us to the stars

The god-like Iaens are infinitely more advanced than humankind, so why have they requested military assistance in a conflict they can surely win unaided?

Torstein Danielson, Secretary for Interplanetary Affairs, is on a fact-finding mission to their home planet and headed straight into the heart of a war-zone. With him, onboard the Starship *Kissinger*, is a detachment of marines for protection, an embedded pack of sycophantic journalists who are not expected to cause trouble, and reporter Katherina Molale, who most certainly will and is never afraid to dig for the truth.

Torstein wants this mission over as quickly as possible. His daughter is terminally ill, his marriage in tatters. But then the Iaens offer a gift in return for military intervention and suddenly the stakes, both for humanity as a race and for Torstein personally, are very high indeed.

ISBN: 9781911409960 (epub, kindle) / 9781911409861 (96pp paperback)

Visit bit.ly/Interference-Grimwood

Stray Pilot

Douglas Thompson

A passionate environmental allegory

Thomas Tellman, an RAF pilot who disappeared pursuing a UFO in 1948, unexpectedly returns entirely un-aged to a small town on Scotland's north-east coast. He finds that his 7-year-old daughter is now a bed-bound 87-year-old woman suffering from dementia. She greets him as her father but others assume she is deluded and that Thomas is an unhinged impostor or con man. While Thomas endeavours to blend in to an ordinary life, his presence gradually sets off unpredictable consequences, locally, nationally and globally. Members of the British Intelligence Services attempt to discredit Thomas in advance of what they anticipate will be his public disclosure of evidence of extra-terrestrial activity, but the local community protect him. Thomas, appalled by the increase in environmental damage that has occurred in his 80 year absence, appears to have returned with a mission: whose true nature he guards from everyone around him.

Douglas Thompson's thought-provoking novel is unashamedly science-fiction yet firmly in the tradition of literary explorations of the experience of the outsider. He weaves together themes of memory loss and dementia, alienation, and spiritual respect for the natural world; while at the same time counterposing the humanity inherent in close communities against the xenophobia and nihilistic materialism of contemporary urban society. Of all the book's vivid characters, the fictional village of Kinburgh itself is the stand-out star: an archetypal symbol of human community. In an age of growing despair in the face of climate crises, *Stray Pilot* offers a passionate environmental allegory with a positive message of constructive hope: a love song to all that is best in ordinary people.

ISBN: 9781915304131(epub, kindle) / 97819153041032 (264pp paperback)

Visit bit.ly/StrayPilot

HARPAN'S WORLDS:
WORLDS APART

TERRY JACKMAN

If Harp could wish, he'd be invisible.

Orphaned as a child, failed by a broken system and raised on a struggling colony world, Harp's isolated existence turns upside down when his rancher boss hands him into military service in lieu of the taxes he cannot pay. Since Harp has spent his whole life being regarded with suspicion, and treated as less, why would he expect his latest environment to be any different? Except it is, so is it any wonder he decides to hide the 'quirks' that set him even more apart?

Space opera with a paranormal twist, Terry Jackman's novel explores prejudice, corruption, and the value of true friendship.

Terry Jackman is a mild-mannered married lady who lives in a quiet corner of the northwest of England, a little south of Manchester. Well, that's one version.

The other one may be a surprise to those who only know the first. [She doesn't necessarily tell everything.] Apart from once being the most qualified professional picture framer in the world, which accounted for over ten years of articles, guest appearances, seminars, study guides and exam papers both written and marked, she chaired a national committee for the Fine Art Trade Guild, and read 'slush' for the *Albedo One* SF magazine in Ireland. Currently she is the coordinator of all the British Science Fiction Association's writers' groups, called Orbits, and a freelance editor.

ISBN: 9781915304179 (epub, kindle) / 97819153041070 (320pp paperback)

Visit bit.ly/HarpansWorldsWorldsApart

You might also enjoy

GALAXIES AND FANTASIES

A Collection of Rather Amazing and Wide-ranging Short Stories

ANDY MCKELL

Prepare for the unexpected

Galaxies and Fantasies is an eclectic collection of tales from master-storyteller Andy McKell, crossing genres from mythology to cosmology, fairytale to space opera, surrealism to hyper-reality. What they all have in common is a twist, a surprise, a revelation. Leave your pre-conceptions aside when you read these stories, prepare for the unexpected, the extraordinary, the unpredictable. Some are quite succinct and you'll be immediately wanting more; others are more elaborate, but deftly devised, and you'll be thinking about them long after you've finished reading. These are stories that will stay with you, not in a haunting way, but like a satisfying memory that often returns to encourage, enchant or enrich your life.

ISBN: 9781915304162 (epub, kindle) / 97819153041063 (186pp paperback)

Visit bit.ly/GalaxiesAndFantasies

About Terry Grimwood

Suffolk born and proud of it, Terry Grimwood is the author of a handful of novels and novellas, including *Deadside Revolution*, the science fiction-flavoured political thriller *Bloody War*, and *Joe* which was inspired by true events. His short stories have appeared in numerous magazines and anthologies and have been gathered into three collections, *The Exaggerated Man*, *There Is A Way To Live Forever* and *Affairs of a Cardio-Vascular Nature*. Terry has also written and Directed three plays as well as co-written engineering textbooks for Pearson Educational Press. He loves music and plays harmonica, and growls songs into a microphone with The Ripsaw Blues Band. Happily semi-retired, he nonetheless continues to teach electrical installation at a further education college. He is married to Debra, the love of his life.

Ingram Content Group UK Ltd.
Milton Keynes UK
UKHW012007160523
421856UK00001B/30